Prey of the Vampire King

THE VAMPIRE KINGS
BOOK FOUR

RHIANNON FUTCH

Contents

One

Valdís

Setting down my morning brew I look around the table. Our breakfast table has been replaced, it just wasn't big enough anymore. Even Epaphras takes his breakfast with us now, too many decisions get made at this table that he needs to be a part of for him to skip it. "I think we need a different place to practice."

Malic looks at me, "Why?"

Sighing I gesture at the huge hole in the wall that happened yesterday. It was an accident but still. Epaphras nods, "I think she is right. We should give them one of the castles. We are overrun with witches right now. There have been three accidental fires this week, and five rooms flooded. Not to mention the small tornado that was let loose in the kitchen. Cook is not ok. He has a twitch."

Knox says, "I think I can speak for all of us when I say that we are not comfortable with the idea of you being in a different castle than we are in."

Chance raises a brow, "I think it's a good idea. This is the castle they always go after, because it is our stronghold. Because we are always here. So, if all the witches take over one of the other castles it could keep them out of harms way. And, we don't all have to be on duty all the time. We could take turns. That way, at least one of us can make sure we are with her at all times."

Malic shakes his head, "I don't like it. It splits our forces and leaves her open to attack. One of us can be overwhelmed. All of us can be overwhelmed, but it takes a lot more people to overwhelm us. This is our stronghold."

I open my mouth to tell them exactly what I think, but Chance starts talking first, "I would like to point out that our "stronghold" has been breached numerous times. And you are completely discounting the fact that our princess is not exactly a damsel in distress anymore. She has power, beyond our capabilities. You are completely ignoring the fact that just yesterday you were too pushy and she left you hanging mid-air. She could just as well have opened a portal under you and dropped you where ever she wanted."

"I like that idea. I think I am going to keep it in reserve for next time you all discuss my safety in front of me while behaving as though I haven't got the ability to do anything to protect myself. Knox, I am not the woman you told to perforate someone. Malic, I am not the woman you met that was too scared to tell you that she was super turned on by you. I'm not even the same woman that Chance met, though she is closer to who I am now than the two before her. Also, I have been taken directly from this castle. Almost taken a couple more times from this castle. We are going to practice elsewhere. The question is will you be a part of that or are we going to fight about it?"

Knox and Malic share a look even as Chance smirks and I know I've convinced them. Malic says, "The north castle is relatively isolated, was built well, and should work for your purposes while being far enough away from people that it should be safe."

Knox nods in agreement, "We'll have to go take it out of lockdown, but it should work well."

With a grin I say, "Excellent! Dagma, Katerine, Kalina, want to go look around with me?"

Dagma nods, trying to keep her smile muted, "I think that would be wonderful. We should bring Quorin and some of the others. That first woman you found, what was her name again?"

"Bettina. She does seem to have really blossomed since she got here. I guess not being continually pursued by some jackass that won't take no for an answer does really good things for a person."

Kalina nods, "Or knowing that he is dead under a rock and can never bother you again..."

I can't help but laugh at the memory of that. Chance was so annoyed by the whole thing. Meeting his eyes I see he is smiling about it too. Knox says, "I suppose if we are all finished, we can go now."

"Yes, let me go get Quorin and Bettina," Epaphras says as he stands, "I believe they are in the library studying now."

～

It isn't long before we are all loaded up and on our way through the tunnels. We reach the end, where a garage should be and there is only wall. Malic gets out and walks over to the wall on the left. Placing his hand flat against it briefly and lifting it away as a panel opens. The panel reveals a small square with buttons. He taps certain buttons and the wall before us starts moving silently into the ground. It is fully concealed again by the time Malic is back in the vehicle.

I've seen them using a lot of interesting little gadgets that I don't think the rest of our land has any idea exist, this being just the latest example. "Where did you get all this stuff? Why doesn't anyone else have any of these things?"

I watch as my kings share a look before Malic shrugs and says, "We have been visiting the outsider's lands for quite some time. Originally it was to ease the boredom and just kind of make sure they thought we didn't exist still. But we realized pretty fast that as our little continent was cut off from the rest of the world it wasn't growing a whole lot. Being as the rest of the world was progressing at a pretty fast pace, we started bringing little bits here. And then as we realized how useful the technology could be... well, we started bringing more. And we shared little bits that could be made to work here. Our phones only work because they are a special kind, we don't have the right setup for the usual kind to work here. Now, we have been watching and keeping up with them on a smaller scale. I have concerns about where some parts of the tech they created have led, but all I can do is hope Hekate protects us if they go that route. The fact that they cannot find us keeps me more at ease with that."

"I want to learn more about this. Where would I find information? Do you have it here? I saw a spell I kind of want to try."

They all give me side-eye about that as we come to a stop in the garage for this castle. Epaphras and the others pull up next to us and we all exit the vehicles. The elevator is a little crowded but manageable. Stepping out of the garage I get my first look at the castle. It is so near the ocean I can smell the salt and hear the waves crash. The walls are high and smooth. But the castle itself takes my breath away. It is built of giant stones, carved and set just so. They show the wear of the ages in a way that the main castle doesn't. There is a quiet, determined strength in this place and I love it already. Looking to my fellow witches I see that same love reflected on their faces.

Quorin says, "I want to live here."

My kings smile, and Chance says, "Then you will need to choose a room."

She blushes and looks to Lommán and back before saying, "Would it, erm, would it be..." she closes her eyes and takes a breath, "Can Lommán move with me?"

My jaw drops at first, I had no idea they were dating! Even as Malic says it is her space, she can have whoever she wants live in it with her a grin spreads across my face. Dagma and I reach them at the same time and she says, "Why did you keep this secret? I am so happy for you both!"

They both blush and Quorin says, "I wasn't ready to

share. He wanted to tell everyone the minute he convinced me. I didn't want you all to worry about what if it didn't work out. And then there just wasn't a good time to tell you, till now."

We both hug them, and congratulate them on finding each other. Knox says, "How about a tour so you can pick a room?"

Quorin lights up and takes Lommán's hand saying, "Yes please."

Gage

I see my brother's boats as I cruise slowly into the harbor. I can't recall the last time four of us were here at one time. Once Vincent arrives it will be the first time the five of us have been on the island together since the murders. As my boat slowly glides into place at its dock, a guard jumps over with a mooring line. They have it moored by the time I finish shutting everything down and are already at the task of unloading the pallets of supplies I brought. I walk across the plank and down onto the dock to look around. Why is there an odd ring on the ground around the castle? "Hey, why is that there?"

The guard looks very nervous as he says, "There was a plant growing there for a while. Excuse me, I need to get this loaded."

The guard nearly runs to get back to the unloading. I don't like it. "I am going to go through the garage and get a bike. I'll see you all at the castle."

A different guard says, "The castle is in lockdown mode. The only way in is through the tunnels. We can stop and let you out at the underground garage if you want to ride a bike instead of with us."

Nodding I look back at the castle. Why is it in lock down? Malic was exaggerating when he said we were under attack, wasn't he? Is this why I needed to bring all these supplies? I thought maybe we were having spoilage issues... It can't be happening again? No way the island would turn against a second time after they murdered our brothers. The guards have finished loading and one calls to me that they are ready to leave when I am. Turning away from the view of the castle I stride over to the vehicle. They left the front passenger seat open for me. Thanking them I get into the seat and wait as the ramp to the tunnels lowers. They drive slow down it, probably concerned about jostling the supplies. It is only moments after we get into the tunnels that the vehicle stops before the door to the other garage. The guard gets out as I do and he touches the wall to open the panel and enter the code. Lock down. The door glides open and I walk in, as I get to a bike I smell... something. It's faint but smells delicious. I want to find it but the scent is old and I know whatever it is, it isn't here. Shaking my head I get the bike checked and wheel it through the door. The guard busies himself with closing it all again while I start the bike.

With one last wave I take off, going much faster than they will. Of course, it takes a lot more to kill me than it does them. Unwelcome memories of my brothers mutilated bodies parade through my mind. Luckily I am slowing to pull into the garage for the main castle when I shake my head to clear the images. Shaking my head to clear it at high speeds has not had good results before and while I healed, it took a long damn time and my suit was ruined.

In this garage the scent is stronger. Much stronger. It awakens a primal side of me, a side that not even my brothers know about. Only our Goddess knows and well, she isn't speaking to any of us. Still. Rolling my shoulders I calm the beast inside, shoving it back down. I must find out what that scent is.

Emerging from the above ground portion of the garage I see the castle we spent many long years building. I want to turn and run back to my boat.

Instead I cross the courtyard and walk in. That scent is everywhere inside the castle and every moment I am tormented with it my control grows weaker, my mood more sour. Finally I find Epaphras, "Where are my brothers? What is that damnable scent? And more importantly, why the hell do I need to be here?"

Epaphras raises his brows at my vehemence. Then lifts his hands and ticks the answers off on his fingers, "They are at lunch with Valdís. The scent is probably Valdís. Because the Outsiders are back."

I am ready to explode until the last one. "What do you mean the Outsiders are back?"

He continues on in the direction he was going before I stopped him. Leaving me to follow as he says, "Well, I don't know that there is more than one way to take that. They are back and actively working to take over the land. So far they have tried to poison us multiple times, thankfully we haven't had as many deaths as could have resulted from that. There were attacks, an attempted election. The last attack came with the election, it was a bit more serious, though stopped before the fighting actually started. But without Valdís, I don't know if it would have gone..." he shakes his head and continues, "It went well. Very few people died and none of those were Atlanteans. There are some lords that appear to be missing now. We haven't searched very hard for them yet as they were part of the attacking force. Oh! Good! Your brothers are going to be very happy about this one!"

I look to where he is pointing at a man being brought in by some guards. He is unkempt and it doesn't appear that he was ever terribly interested in hygiene. At my questioning look Epaphras continues, "He is one of the people that participated in getting poison into the castle. Perhaps I should let Cook have a visit with him before your brothers get back. He is still very angry about the whole mess. When his helper died... he hasn't quite recovered from that. He takes his responsibility for them all very seriously. He insisted that he be allowed to tell the family. The crown paid all the expenses and your brothers attended the burial. They gave the family a permanent stipend to cover the income they lost with their son. The family is one of the farming families and they bring food here every week. But you must want to change and freshen up after the long trip. Your room is ready and your brothers should be back soon with Valdís."

Valdís

I decided to go back to the castle with my kings after lunch. Quorin and Lommán are absolutely adorable but still somewhat uncomfortable about being open with their relationship in front of everyone. Or at least they seem that way to me. I really want to give them time and not hinder the blossoming of their relationship into the rest of the world. I thought perhaps giving them some time alone for now would be the considerate thing to do.

I should ask her though. Or Lommán. I shouldn't assume. What if I made them feel like I wasn't comfortable? Oh geez. I will talk to her tomorrow. If I go back right now I am just going to seem weirder than usual. No one needs to spend their time concerned with whether or not the most powerful witch of our time is losing her damn mind.

As we are walking through the castle this scent hits me and I stop walking to take it in as my eyes drift closed. When I open them I see Epaphras trailing behind a man.

The man is dressed in a suit, pressed and tailored. He looks expensive and deadly.

He stops and lifts his nose, I watch his chest swell as he inhales. His eyes are golden and they flash as he zeroes in on me. I feel his gaze on me and I want him with a ferocity that frightens me. His demeanor changes, he starts moving toward me and I am suddenly just as terrified as I am turned on. Chance grabs me and shoves me behind his body, holding me there when my traitorous body tries to lead me to my doom.

Knox and Malic block the hall, but the man is still trying to walk through them, his gaze focused solely on me, like he can't see anything else. The fear from my kings is just scaring me more. I remember what saying the Goddess's name does the first time a person hears it and I try to shout it, but my throat is clenched in fear. Clearing my throat I try again, "Hekate! Hekate! Hekate!"

The man drops into unconsciousness between one breath and the next, Knox and Malic holding him up to keep him from hitting the floor. As my brain comes back online I take a deep breath and say, "Let me guess, King Gage?"

Chance chuckles, "Yes. That's Gage. He's always been a little intense. I guess that the scent of you hit him pretty hard."

Chance keeps an arm around me as we follow behind Knox and Malic. Epaphras looks around and announces that he is going elsewhere as he does not want to be there when King Gage wakes. He exits the room as they lay Gage on a couch, arranging him so he can rest comfortably.

Chance offers to stay with him and be there when he wakes up. Knox smiles, "I think maybe it would be better if he wakes up to us. You are more like him, more feral. The castle has been through enough lately. No, we'll stay." He says pointing at himself and then Malic.

Malic nods, "I agree. Take Valdís to her room and the two of you should have dinner in there too. I think it might be a little while before we get him convinced to act right."

Chance nods and tries to steer me out of the room. I slip out of his arms and go to Knox, hugging him. Raising up onto my toes I whisper to him, "Thank you."

He squeezes me lightly and pulls me away to put his hands on either side of my face, "We are always here for you, however you need us." He kisses me softly on the lips before releasing me.

Going to Malic I do the same, hugging him and thanking him. He kisses me hard as he crushes my body to his. When he sets me back down I am a little unsteady in the nicest of ways. On the couch Gage twitches in his sleep and I flinch. Great.

Moving to Chance's side I take his arm and ask, "Ready to go?"

Cardinal Francis

"Where are the men that were supposed to be guarding the facility?"

The man before me twitches like he wants to fidget but is restraining himself, if only barely. "We don't know. Their car is gone, they haven't been to their home since they left for work that day. Our search of the rubble did not reveal their bodies either."

"Did our background research not reveal that these men were orphans and ideal for recruitment as they were in dire straights and had no one to turn to? How is it possible that a few..." my lip curls as I spit the word out, "witches, convinced them to help in a destructive escape of this magnitude? The entire building is rubble!"

"Your Eminence, we feel certain that they were not alone. Other cameras in the area showed unusual activity around the building. It appears that a small military force set the charges around the building."

"Leave me. I need to pray on this."

Standing as the man leaves the room I curse this body that just keeps aging. Time is running out. If I don't get the witches magic soon it won't matter anymore.

Kneeling painfully at the altar to my God, I pick up the matches. Lighting a candle and dousing the match in a bowl of sand kept for that purpose.

"First, let me say again that the kneeling cushion is greatly appreciated. The damned witches we had have escaped and my man tells me that a military force probably helped them. How did they get a military? They're just some witches!"

I quake on my cushion when my God's voice echos in the room, "What witches escaped with military help? Tell me everything."

I quietly tell him everything that happened, from the moment we first found her stealing our witches from our land to the conversation I just had with my man. When his laughter booms in my quiet room I only just manage to keep from covering my ears. He hates it when I do that and gets so much louder. When he is done laughing he tells me, "The key has finally been revealed. It is a glorious time for you to be alive. Your task now is to put together a team."

"A team?"

"Yes. An extraction team. The witch you caught stealing the other witches, she is the key. You get your team put together, only the best for this mission. Get them together, brief them on who they are after and that she is a witch. Have them light my candle and call me when they are on the boat. I will open the way for them to where she is. When they have her and leave, the way home will be shortened as well. Choose well, it will be on you if they fail to collect my key."

I feel the absence when he leaves even as I watch the candle extinguish itself. Struggling up from the kneeling cushion I cross the room to the door. Opening it I tell the man outside, "Send my guard master in."

Three

CHANCE

No sooner than we exit the room I scoop her up in my arms. She protests as I walk saying, "You are aware that I can walk?"

Grinning at her I say, "Fully aware." My smile fades as I tell her, "I am also very aware of just how devious and dogged Gage can be. He wasn't fully in control there but he was very determined to get to you. He looks like the most civilized of us all with his suits and boardroom life. It only mostly conceals the fact that he is the most feral of us. I am carrying you because I will get us in your much more defensible room a lot faster than we could with you walking. And, I might want to have you all to myself in your room for as long as possible."

She giggles at the last remark. Right then we arrive at the door to her room and I lower her legs to the floor. She looks around, "Well, I guess you did get us here faster." She opens the door and steps in, "be welcomed to my domain good sir."

I never thought being welcomed into a room would be something that turned me on, but here we are, my dick waking up and reminding me that we haven't had any time alone since we came back home. She shuts and locks the door behind me, when I turn and look back with a raised brow she says, "I know a locked door won't necessarily stop you all, but you do usually try the handle first. So I figure it buys us a few seconds more if he makes it here."

Chuckling I tell her, "You aren't wrong, we do generally try the usual way of opening a door first." Her face changes then, she looks very intense as she starts walking toward me. "Everything ok?"

She smiles, "I have suddenly realized that I have you all alone." She reaches me and puts her hands on my shoulders. My heart rate picks up and my cock swells further. She leans in to whisper near my ear, "Care to finish what we started before we came home?"

Swallowing, I nod as my voice seems to be gone for the moment. She gently pushes me back across the room, till my legs hit her bed. Her hands on my shoulders give a little push and I sit. Then this gorgeous dark beauty kneels before me and starts working the laces on my boots. I move to help and she gently pushes my hands away. She makes quick work of getting my boots off. Raising up on her knees she grabs the bottom edge of my shirt, tugging it up and off of me. She stands and pulls me up to stand, her hands going to my chest and gliding down to the fastening of my pants. I think I may have forgotten to breathe as she unfastens and pushes them down till they drop. I can feel the warmth from her body, so close. Straightening, she leans in and nips my neck before whispering, "Get in the bed and I'll let you watch me undress."

I have never leapt to obey in my life like I did for that offer.

Laying back in the middle of this huge bed, I watch as she kicks off her shoes. Her hands go to her waist, fingers slipping under the bottom edge of her shirt. She lifts it so slowly, her glorious skin revealed a bare inch at a time. The underside of her breasts come into view and I see she hasn't been wearing a bra all day. Her nipples are large and rosy brown, I want to take them in my mouth and suck them till she can't see straight. She drops the shirt on the floor and her hands go the waist band of her skirt. I am transfixed as she slips her thumbs under it and pushes downward. The patch of curls are exposed to my gaze and I realize she hasn't been wearing anything underneath her clothing this whole day.

She drops the skirt and steps out of it, a bronze goddess come to life. I watch her lift a leg and step onto the bed. Her hips sway with every step she takes toward me. She stops, one foot on either side on my knees. She lowers herself to a crouch and then rocks forward, smoothly dropping her knees on either side of my hips. Putting her hands on my shoulders she moves her knees forward till her core is hovering over my cock. I am throbbing with need, my hips twitching with the urge to bury myself in her nearly overwhelming. Then she lowers herself onto my lap, my cock pressed lengthwise against the heat of her. She rocks her hips and I groan, my hips rocking of their own volition. She sucks air through her teeth as her nails bite into my shoulders.

Her voice low she says, "I had ideas of drawing this out but I don't think I can. I need you inside me Chance." I don't have the air to respond so my hands release the blanket I hand a death grip on and go to her hips, lifting her as I rock my hips down. My eyes roll back as my cock lines up with her hot, slick core. My brain only just comprehends it when she says, "Go slow, Chance. Please."

She moans as I lower her slowly, I have to pause a moment and breathe, she feels so fucking good. A little lower, her hips are twitching in my hands, her nails digging into my shoulders. Lower still and she moans, I can't take it and I thrust upward. I feel the tremor run through her body.

We both hold still for long moments, just trying to breathe. Then her hips start to rock and I open my eyes to watch this woman, my queen, take possession of my soul. Those big beautiful nipples are just inches from my face and I can't resist. Leaning forward I take one in my mouth, sucking hard. She moans and presses forward as her hips start rocking faster. Sliding my hand in toward her clit I get my thumb in place so that she is rubbing against it as her hips rock.

She cries out, her hips rocking faster. It's all I can do to hold on. I watch as she hits her peak and cries out again as her core starts clenching around my cock. Her movements slow and I roll us over so she is on her back. One hand on her hips and the other still on her clit, I draw back slowly till only the head is still sheathed within her. Pressing her clit with my thumb I start pounding into her. Her eyes fly open as she says, "Goddess yes! Fuck me!"

That is all the invitation I need. Driving my cock into her over and over till she convulses against me again and I can't hold back this time, emptying myself into her with one last thrust.

∾

Gage

The darkness begins to recede and before it is gone the memories pour in like a dam suddenly crumbled into nothing. Hekate visiting me in my penthouse in the lands of the Outsiders. Her suggestion is why I still hunt the Organization even now. So much was wiped away. She told me it would help me protect her. I was so mad about the fairy tale of a queen that I actually told her I was too old to need fairy tales. She slapped me, appearing suddenly as the dark and terrifying Hekate from the tales of old as she told me that the Goddess Hekate tells no fairy tales, if I wanted those I could join the Outsiders. I apologized once I had picked myself up off the floor. Just as quickly she was back to our Hekate, she told me she understood my discontent. She took my hand and said, "I have a gift for you." She waved a hand toward the interior of my place and an image of a woman appeared. She was curvaceous, with long dark hair and dark olive skin. Hekate told me the woman would save us all.

I snorted, "She's so frail, one fall and those pretty bones are smashed."

Hekate laughed at me, "Dear one, not all strength is in the arms. Her heart, her heart is so strong. That is where her strength lies, that beautifully strong heart is going to be the key to everything. Once you all have accepted her and she accepts you all, she will never waver and she won't abandon you. If we lose her, we are all of us doomed."

That is when my eyes snap open and I sit up to see Knox and Malic watching me closely, "Where is she? Is she safe? We can't lose her."

Knox and Malic exchange looks before Malic tells me, "She is safe. Tell me about you. Are you safe for her now?"

"Yes. I want her, just as much as I did in the hall. But I remember it all now. It isn't me she needs to fear. Hekate showed me what she would look like, before she hid my memories from me."

Knox nods, "Yes, she did that to all of us. I know she had her reasons, but it isn't the most pleasant thing ever. I guess she was well aware that you wouldn't be the first one to see her and that your reaction would be... intense."

I look at the floor, "Yes. She does inspire a certain intensity in the reaction to her scent. Does it get easier to be around her?"

Malic nods, "It does. Knowing that she is the source of the scent helps. Being around her more and being intimate with her does more to calm the craving than anything. I don't know how long it will be before she is willing in your case. It's been different with each of us. I think Chance may have fought harder against believing she is the queen longer than any of us."

"She's more than the queen."

Knox eyes me, "What do you mean more than the queen?"

Shrugging I tell him, "She is just more, I can't explain it. I understood it when Hekate explained it. I still understand it. I don't know if it is something I would be allowed to explain. It feels like my throat wants to close when I think about explaining it. She's just more."

Knox chuckles, "I don't suppose we need to know more than that."

Four

Eumeleia

We decided that we should stop by my house first. When I walk in Flaviana immediately comes running at me. "Your mother is gone! Have you seen her anywhere? She hasn't returned since she left the field in front of the castle! I am so worried for her!"

"No, I haven't seen her. That is worrisome." What could have happened to her? I heard the rumors that she rode away, and I am sure she did. Did she go into hiding? That must be it. "I'm sure she is fine and will come back when she is able. It is likely she didn't want to bring the wrath of the kings down on the entire house. Come, show me what is needing a decision here." I know Flaviana is mother's favorite employee, and therefore the one that she tasks with most everything. It doesn't take us long to go through the few things that mother would have made decisions on. My darling Pelos walks with us the entire time, completely encouraging of my taking charge of the household in my mother's absence.

On the way back toward the front door I tell Flaviana, "Now, I must get going."

"But ma'am! You just arrived!"

"I am aware of that Flaviana. What you are not aware of is that I have just come back from marrying my dear Pelos and we are on our way to his home. We stopped in to make the announcement to mother, but as she isn't here, do let us know if she comes home. And, keep our marriage a surprise. I want to tell her myself." Mostly because I want to see her face when she finds out he won't be forced into marrying Valdís of all people, but Flaviana doesn't need to know that. "Until she comes back I will come by every week to check on things. Keep things going as they should and if the house money needs replenished, do let me know. I will expect to see an accounting for the money used."

Flaviana's face falls as I tell her my plans, I am unsure if that is due to her wanting me here or due to my expectations of accounting. It doesn't matter though. She'll take care of things here.

Pelos and I take our leave, the drive to his home is short. He opens the vehicle door for me and holds my hand to steady me as I get out. I yelp in surprise as he lifts me off my feet, "Pelos! What are you doing?"

He laughs, "I am carrying my bride over the threshold. Watch, Hulthen will open the door for us even."

As he predicted, the door opens and Hulthen is holding it as he carries me through and sets me down gently.

Hulthen is much more subdued as he says, "Sir, about your father..."

Pelos nods, "He hasn't been home, has he? We've just been at Eumeleia's family home, Eirene hasn't been home either. I dare say they are likely in hiding for concern about the king's wrath. Have you been leaving notes on his desk in his absence, as usual?" Hulthen nods and Pelos continues, "Then I will go tend to answering what needs taken care of. And Hulthen, Eumeleia and myself are recently married, you will treat her requests as though they came from myself or my father, understood?" Hulthen's eyes widen just a hair, barely noticeable. He nods and Pelos turns to me, taking my hand, "Come, let's go work on our household decisions together." We walk toward his father's office together and I think I just couldn't be happier than I am right now.

Inside his father's office Pelos says, "I am a bit concerned as all the news we have heard from him is that he was unconscious on the field last anyone saw him and now he is gone. I have to wonder if he isn't rotting in the dungeon."

"Well, he could be in hiding with my mother. Perhaps we should send a message to the castle to inquire if they are as they haven't been home? We weren't there so it isn't like they will be after us. Our parent's gave us the blessing of not being involved in their schemes over much. Goddess knows, mother has plans for me." I laugh, "She wanted me to marry one of the kings."

Pelos looks up from the notes on his father's desk, "Was that something you wanted? To marry a king?"

"No! The kings are not for me. I never dreamed of marrying royalty. I always dreamed of marrying my father's best friend's son. He was a handsome rake even when we were children." I smile over at my husband who is grinning now, "Spoiled me for everyone else."

"Good, because he has always dreamed of you too." Pelos finishes the notes and starts opening the drawers in his father's desk.

Walking over to stand next to him I ask, "What are you doing?"

"Satisfying my curiosity. My father has always been very particular about his desk and it has never failed to strike me as odd. He would rather come get something himself than allow someone in his desk."

"Well that is odd, considering the little I know about your father."

"It is," he says as he opens another drawer and starts carefully going through it. His face changes as he pulls out a small box, the top is an embossed skull and crossbones. The universal symbol for poison. His face twists with pain and hate as he turns the box over in his hands, opening it and smelling it. "I know this smell! This is what the morning tea smelled like. The same morning tea that my father started making for my mother when she got sick!" He stands abruptly, the chair falling back to land with a crash. He slams the container down on the desk, powder spilling to cover the papers he just went through. "How could I have been such a damn fool? He killed her right in front of us all!" He shouts and rages, it is frightening and I can't help but shrinking back. Until his anger runs dry and the tears for his mother 's life begin to flow. The sobs are wracking and heartbreaking to hear as I go to him, wrapping my arms around him. His arms go round me and nearly crush me to him as he cries. Sobbing out, "I'm so sorry mother, I didn't realize. How could he do this? How could he take you from us?"

I rub his back in small circles as he cries himself out. His sobs grow softer and his grip eases. Finally he releases me and leans back, "I am so sorry to have unmanned myself before you my love. I was taken by surprise."

"Pelos," I cup his cheek with a hand, "my love, you are not unmanned for having emotions. Finding out your father poisoned your mother is an emotional experience to say the least. You never need be ashamed of having emotions before me. I confess to having fears about what sort of father yours has been for you all these years that you would hide even the emotions from finding your mother was poisoned."

He smiles a little lopsidedly, "He is a very hard man, with no emotions to speak of beyond anger and greed. And now we know his hatred of my mother went so deep he felt that he must murder her."

"Well, my love, what shall we do about this? Will we pretend not to know? Will we turn him in? What do you want to do?"

"I need to think about this." He looks at the powder clinging to his hands, "And I want to clean this up so that none of it touches you. I couldn't bear to lose you now. He walks back to the desk and carefully picks up the box, taking the lid fully off and tapping it against the top edge of the bottom half to release any of the powder clinging to the top. I watch him carefully dust as much of the powder as possible back into the container.

"Could you open the door, my love? I think I need to wash this from my hands."

Five

KNOX

"It has to be women. The men of this land have proven again and again that they are easily swayed by their own sense of importance and greed. Here in the castle right now are the vast majority of the witches that have always lived on our land. They have come to stay in the castle and haven't gone back to their husbands or families. That's why we have had at least two incidents a week of men trying to take the women they feel they own back from us. The document has to specify women, and it has to include those that were not recognized as women at birth."

"Sire, this is going to cause an uproar. The men here are barely ok with you lot ruling them, what are they going to do when you tell them that you plan to put the women in charge?"

"Obey if they know what is good for them. You know what, pretty much every woman that is from this island is a witch. That is the requirement. Must be a witch to be on the council. And we are going to make laws before we step down, laws that protect the women in ways we were too damn dumb to notice were needed."

"I hardly think you are dumb for being unaware of a problem sire."

"We are though. Because we could have if we had paid a modicum of attention to the prevalence of the petitions for protection. Do you know how many we have had in the past year? Do you? I checked, and it is horrifying. There were over a thousand in the past year alone. Which is seven times the amount of land grievance petitions, which were the next largest number. Seven times Epaphras! We are dumb and we haven't paid nearly enough attention to our world. We were all so absorbed in our own misery we never bothered to worry for our people. This is where things change. And if I have to slaughter half her people myself to make them act right about this, so be it. I think she will allow it for this."

Epaphras sighs, "It may well come to that. Are you sure your brothers will go along with all this?"

"I am. None of us ever wanted to rule. Vincent least of all. I think he will leap at the chance." I turn to look at him, pausing my pacing, "We are warriors, and maybe some other things that we haven't been happy enough to pursue. Perhaps, perhaps if we can make this work we can finally do that. Now that..."

He nods, "I think I begin to understand. So the council is to be witches only. And we know because of Quorin that regardless of what people label them at birth, Hekate knows who they are and her women are witches so no worries that we would be excluding any women in that way."

"Exactly! And that will keep it at only women from our land, no outsiders are ever going to be witches. Hekate won't allow it."

"I need some time with one of our legal team to get this worded correctly."

"Very well, put the document draft in the safe under the plant there. Do not let them see you remove it from that safe. Only one of them and be certain that they will not try to wrk against this or tell the rest of the island before we are ready to reveal a final document."

"Certainly. Anything else?"

"Possibly, but I have some things to tend to for now."

"Excellent. I'll put this away and go do some other things myself while I ponder which of the legal team will be right for this job. Now that I think about it, I do have one other thing."

"Yes?"

"Remember when we sent the guards out for the vendor that orchestrated the poisoning?"

"Oh yes! Is he here?"

Epaphras looks a little nervous. Did he get away? Epaphras tugs on his collar, "Well, physically yes. The thing is, I told Cook that he could go speak to the man first. He, well, I never expected... When I went down to the dungeons later I found that Cook had carved him up."

"Oh? Well, that's fine. I don't mind leftovers."

Epaphras sighs, "Sire, he carved the entire man up. The vendor is appetizers now."

I feel my eyes go round and inappropriate laughter bubbling up. "Cook turned him into snacks for us?"

"In a manner of speaking, yes? And I do have some good news, the twitch Cook picked up is gone now."

And that breaks me, my laughter echoing through the halls.

Gage

I have to clear her scent from my nose, even if only for a short time. I long to be near her, but she avoids me. I smell her fear, and I can see it when she leaves any room I come into. I hate it, and it angers me. My brothers tell me to wait, to be patient, that I scared even them the day that I came home.

So, when I can't stand breathing in her scent another moment I come out here and stomp around the garden till I feel more calm. Sometimes it takes walking the garden all night before I can go back inside. It is a nice, quiet place of solitude at night. One filled with other scents to permeate my nose.

I am walking through the roses again when I catch a whiff of her. I look around for a place to hide, to be allowed to even observe her. Possibly without bothering her, maybe she won't notice me. I spot a break in the roses, a space for a tree. The deeper shadows under the tree, with the low light of early evening she shouldn't be able to see me. The scent of the roses might even cover up my scent for her.

She walks into the clearing, her eyes on the plants.

Fingers trailing over petals. She is breathtaking. I could watch her for an eternity. She stops and smells a rose. Her eyes drift closed as she breathes in the scent. A finger runs along the edge of the rose as she moves on to the next. She stops mid-step, lifting her face.

She is like the creatures I hunt in the lands of the others. I know she has smelled me when her eyes fly open. The scent of her fear and lust pervades the clearing. Her eyes scan the area and stop on my hiding spot. She calls out to me, surprising her guards, "What are you doing here?"

Stepping forward into the light I tell her, "Walking the gardens, same as you."

She scowls, "It looks more like you are lurking in the dark waiting for someone. you can have the garden. I'll go inside."

I start toward her saying, "Wait, you can st--," and suddenly I am flying through the air to land in one of the rose bushes. The footsteps of her and her guards retreat quickly toward the castle.

Gathering up my dignity, I try to get up and I realize this isn't one of the thornless varieties. Wonderful. Nothing quite so humbling as pulling thorns out of your ass for an hour.

Valdís

I can't believe that man! Always lurking everywhere! Chance did it too, but he wasn't so very frightening. I mean, he was, but not like Gage is. Seeing him in the garden, I can't stand it. That's the garden that I love and go to for solace. For silence.

Instead I find myself hunted. Stalked. Creepers hiding in the damn dark. I can't do this again. I just can't deal with another king with an attitude. I have to keep working on my magic and I can't do that if I am spending all my time scared and horny.

Rounding the corner to the kings bloody wing I head directly for my room. I am not staying here. There is a whole other castle for witches and I am just going to go stay there until I feel better about this whole situation. In my room I turn and look at my guard, "Could you find me a large bag? I am going to go stay at the Witches Keep for a time and I want to take some of my things with me."

His eyes go round and he stammers, "Yes. Certainly." As he leaves I start collecting some clothing and bathing items. Before the pile on my bed is complete my kings come rushing to my side.

Malic pushes to the front, asking, "What happened?"

"Gage was in the gardens. Eyes all golden and looking much more feral than any of you ever did. He feels dangerous in a way that none of you ever did. With all that has happened, I just don't have it in me to deal with whatever issues he needs to work through to act right. I'm going to go stay at the Witches Keep for a while."

Knox sighs, "It won't get better if you avoid him. It is the lure of you that has him acting out."

"And that's the problem! You all act out! Put me through a damn wringer just so you don't have to face some damn thing you haven't handled! It's been three of you already! First you Knox, running hot and cold like a tap on the fritz. Then Malic so afraid that he does his best to scare me away to not have someone else to worry about. And Chance, he seemed to be certain that I was working to betray you all. Fucked if I know what that is even about!" My guard comes in then with a bag that he hands over while eyeing the kings, I take it from him and start shoving things in. "I just need some space. While he works out his own shit. Whatever my destiny may be I can't believe that I am meant to fix your issues and mine. I am going to continue with my studies. I know you aren't necessarily aware Chance, but Malic and Knox know that I have to gain control of my magic or bad things are going to happen. You all are amazing, and maybe Gage is too. But right now I can't see it. I need this. Please tell me you won't fight me on this."

Malic runs his hands over his face, "No. I won't fight you on this. Will you take your guards and one of us at least?"

"Yes. I can do that. I am happy to do that. I am not banishing you all, or even him. I am drawing a boundary. None of you get to be awful beasts to me just because you have issues. Sort yourselves out. I'm not responsible for your neurosis."

Chance asks, "Is there more I don't know?"

Knox laughs, "Of course. We've all been busy with so many things, we certainly didn't stop to catch you up on everything we ever heard from her or found out about her." He chuckles, "Hell, when she got here, she didn't know everything about her."

"He's right. Ok, Well, you three draw straws or something. I'm opening a portal and going." I busy myself with creating the portal while they sort themselves. When I turn to grab my bag I see that my guards have already picked it up, they walk through the portal carrying my bag like they've done it a million times already. Knox and Malic come to kiss me. Knox telling me he will be by to see me tomorrow and Malic telling me he will be by frequently, but don't stay gone for too long. I hug them both, suddenly almost reluctant to leave until I see Gage standing in the doorway to my bedroom. Releasing my kings I turn and walk through my portal, Chance close behind as I go through. I can see Gage still watching me with those golden eyes as I turn back to close the portal.

Malic

Valdís has been gone for two days now. I see her daily, but I miss her scent in the castle. The taste of her on my lips when I see her walking through the castle. I miss her. Just her not being here makes me uneasy. I fear that we will have to give her up if we don't all agree about her.

Whatever happens, she is my queen, whether or not everyone agrees.

I would like to not lose any more of my brothers in the process. I've tried talking to Gage, but he is a tight-lipped bastard if there ever was one. He has been incredibly snarly since she left, perhaps he misses her presence too. Sitting in this office staring at papers I am not seeing isn't helping. I should go check in with Knox, maybe he is seeing this from a different angle.

Leaving my office, I head for the main office. It's where Knox usually does his work. Maybe he has had more success with working than I have had.

Opening the door to his office I find him and Epaphras at work on something, "Am I interrupting?"

Knox turns to me, "Not at all. Remember when we spoke about maybe putting a council in charge? We are working on the documents to put a council of witches in charge."

"So you are working to ensure that it stays only witches. Good. Do you have time to take a break?"

"Of course." He leans himself against the corner of his

desk. Epaphras, sitting behind the desk, sets his pen down on the desk. Knox asks, "What's on your mind?"

"Valdís mostly. But, this situation with Gage is disturbing me too. What if they don't reconcile? Will we have to choose between a brother and our queen? Has he talked to you at all?"

Knox and Epaphras both shake their heads no. Knox crosses his arms over his chest, "Gage has never been very interested in talking. Even before..." he shakes his head, "Valdís doesn't have a lot to say about it either, beyond him scaring her and she doesn't want to deal with whatever his issues are. Personally, I think they will work it out. Gage is smart. Sometimes smarter than either of us. And he remembered her, I don't think he's fighting against her. If anything I think he is fighting to get himself right for her. Do you remember how miserable it was having her scent everywhere before we were accepted?"

"I do."

Epaphras clears his throat, "If I may interject?" I wave for him to go ahead. "Sires, I don't know if you all are aware that every one of you talks to yourself out loud as you walk when you are upset."

Scrunching my face I say, "Well, no I was not aware of that. Why?"

Knox looks equally puzzled as Epaphras says, "Gage has been pacing the castle for a couple days now. You all try to speak to him, I just listen as he walks by. Gage is incredibly worried for what is coming for Valdís. If I understand correctly, he wants to be with her and this separation is hurting him. He also mumbles something about being a beast, but I haven't figured out quite what he means by that."

Knox nods, "There you go, Malic. He is not going to reject her. I feel certain he will get himself sorted and she will accept him. It isn't that she doesn't want him, she didn't say that. She doesn't want to be responsible for fixing him. Honestly, I apologized to her yesterday for putting her through that. Just because we have been waiting for her all this time doesn't mean she is responsible for whatever shit we have going in our heads. Fuck, we've been around this long and we still acted like idiots. She was completely accurate when she said I ran hot and cold, I did. She hated it. And she told me off for it too."

I run a hand through my hair, "Well, I agree with you there. I suppose I am somewhat reassured knowing that he is trying. I just hope he doesn't fail. I don't want to lose any of you for any reason."

Knox crosses the room and puts his hands on my shoulders, "It will work out. Have faith. If nothing else, have faith in Hekate, she sure as shit is not going to let her plans be wrecked by idiocy. Even ours." He pulls me in for a hug that I return, grateful for the comfort. Releasing me he says, "So, is it time for our daily visit yet?"

~

Gage

I regretted everything the instant she ran from me. I've spent the past two days pacing these damnable halls trying to figure out how to fix this. How do I convince her that I am not a danger for her? How do I tell her that I have been in love with her since I first saw her image? That there has been no one else for me since because she already had my heart? That I would tear this world into tiny shreds just to keep her safe?

Hekate pulled her true image from the depths of time when she showed me the woman that would haunt my dreams even when I couldn't recall them. Now, to be so close to her but banished from her presence because I couldn't maintain control over the beast that I am is torture.

I have to figure out a way to show her that I would not hurt her. And if possible, a way to make up for frightening her with my loss of control. Whatever I do, it must be soon.

I know Hekate didn't tell her or my brothers what is coming. I have to keep her safe and the only way I can do that is if she allows me near her. I need to talk to my brothers. I don't like it, because every word between us is another chance for the things they don't know to come to light. It has to be done though. For her. For her I would happily walk through fire to be at her side.

I know they will help me. She is already their queen. She is mine as well, even if she hasn't accepted me just yet. I'll do whatever I must to win her acceptance of me, even if it means I have to beg.

Seven

EIRENE

I can't believe he didn't warn me! You'll learn something important. Yes, of course I will. But a damned warning that it would be about Valdís being a witch and wiping out the majority of our forces with a single damn word would have been nice! Now I am leading a bunch of men, people from my ancestral lands, to the safe house. And the lords. Can't forget the damned lords. Only one or two broke their fool necks falling from their horses when Valdís was speaking, saying her deity's name. The rest were slung over saddles, put on the horses I had waiting on the sidelines. My men were not gentle with them, and I don't care. I feel quite certain that showing my face or theirs anywhere near the castle at this time is going to be nothing more than a death wish fulfilled.

I have no desire to die any time soon.

The house I have saved for just such an occasion is on

the far side of the continent from the kings, to the north and west. Very near our home by the cliff. It really is a shame that the brat didn't die in the water that night. It would have solved so many problems. It has taken so long for us to get here, riding bloody horses the long damn way around. We have made it here though. Dismounting I tell my men, "Get those lords put in the cage and the horses tended. There will be food for you in the kitchen, I warned my people here that they should expect us."

The house is quiet and running as it should when I walk in. Ignoring it all I head directly for my room. Closing the door behind me I call out to my God. "How is this part of the plan? We were defeated before we even got started! All we learned is that my stepdaughter is a damned witch!"

An image of my God appears, "We learned so much more than that. Are you really so blind you cannot see that? I am disappointed in you. The key has revealed herself. Your stepdaughter is no mere witch, she is the key! That is what we learned!"

"The key? The key you have been searching for since before this ridiculous big island had more than stupid barbarians living on it? That key? I had her in my house! I could have trussed her up and brought her to you myself! We could have avoided all of this!"

"Foolish child! There are things in this world that must happen, whether I will them or not! The revealing of the key hidden in time and space was one of them. If you, foolish mortal, had killed her before time it would have defeated us. You who couldn't even manage a child you didn't care for without trying to murder her!" His image grows large and frightening even as his voice is so loud it shakes the rafters. "You are nothing but an idiot mortal and if you continue to behave with so much disrespect you can and will be replaced! Lest you forget, you have a daughter, the line does not end with you."

Dropping to my knees and prostrating myself at his feet I tell him, "I am so sorry! I got carried away with my emotions and forgot my place! Please forgive me!"

I stay there, still as I can be for someone whose insides are somersaulting in fear, until he says, "You may stand. Do not forget your place again." He is silent as I get to my feet. "Now that you are listening, I am sending a team here. They will come ashore soon. You will go meet them at the shoreline. I will let you know when it is time."

"Yes, I will await your word. Thank you."

Ingemar

Everything hurts. As the darkness begins to recede the pain of my body is what takes its place. Chances are the pain is what has interrupted the darkness I was cocooned within. I hear voices. Possibly above me? My eyes seem less than willing to open but they do finally and I see bars. Great. Am I in the dungeons? Rolling to my side and pushing myself up, I look around. This doesn't look quite like the dungeons, but it is a cage. I see my fellow lords in here with me. Well shit, this doesn't bode well no matter who has us. I realize I am still hearing voices and I tune in, trying to focus on what they are saying. It is Eirene! And that voice from her office. It sounds as though she is being told off. Closing my eyes I work to focus my efforts to hear them.

Eirene says, "Yes, I will await your word. Thank you."

The voice is quieter now as it asks, "Is there anything else you need my child?"

"I brought those idiot lords here, but now I am unsure what to do with them. I had my men throw them in the cage, and I could just leave them there to rot. But perhaps we have a use for them?"

Oh fuck. Please have a use for them. Or at least for me, shit. I do not want to die in a cage like this.

The voice replies, "You should keep them for now. They will be useful later. Some may even prove their loyalty, you could keep them on in your retinue when you come home."

"Come home? Am I to be allowed to return home finally?"

"Yes, my child. You will come home with the team. And take your rightful place as queen."

"Oh thank you! Am I to bring the lords with me?"

"Yes."

Well that's a relief. Knowing my life is extended for a bit longer I open my eyes and start to survey my surroundings. It would appear we were tossed in here one at a time, happily they made the effort to not pile us one atop the other. I shudder to think how much being on the bottom of that pile would pain me. I don't see a commode any— oh no. There is a hole in the floor. That's it. I have heard my servants complain after my fellow lords were over. They can't aim their dicks into a toilet properly, there is no way they are hitting that hole even if they kneel over the damn thing.

Fuck.

Eight

Valdís

Chance is already gone from my side when I wake. He has been every morning. Usually I find he has left to visit his brothers while I sleep or train. I don't mind it, it is nice having some time alone when I wake up. This morning though, this morning I have a feeling that I need to do something. Something that has been put off for entirely too long. Something none of my kings will appreciate.

It's time to collect my father's diaries.

Once I am up and moving I ask around for Chance. I could do a spell to find him but I kind of like talking to everyone here and I find out more of what is happening with my witches. They tell me he is in the courtyard training. I wander out to see him beating the hell out of multiple dummies at once. It is really pretty impressive. Calling my magic I lift some sticks from various points around him and send them racing at him. He slashes through each of them with ease and still makes the circuit with his dummies before stopping facing me. "Good morning Valdís, feeling spicy today?"

Laughing, I say, "No, I thought that would be entertaining and a new challenge for you. It was, wasn't it?"

He smiles as he walks toward me. The smooth grace of his body is stunning every time I see it. He snatches his shirt from the back of a bench as he walks toward me, using it to wipe the sweat from his body. I could watch this for a while. He threads his fingers through my hair and pulls me in for kiss that lights up my entire body. He breaks the kiss, murmuring, "We could go back upstairs and start the morning over again."

"I actually wanted to talk to you. And your brothers. It's time for me to collect my father's diaries."

He looks puzzled, "Your father's diaries? Where are they? Do I know about this?"

"Maybe? Whether or not you know about this, it still has to happen. I need to go to my father's office in the barn on my property and collect his diaries."

"Ok, can you wait long enough for me to change clothes?"

"Yes." I grin at him, "If you hurry. I am starting for the garage now."

He is gone before I finish my sentence, racing to change his clothes. I walk toward the garage and try to forget that I could easily win this by opening a portal. Probably better if they mostly forget about my portal abilities until I need them. He appears next to me as I enter the garage and I laugh, "You're getting slow."

He grins and shakes his head, spraying water everywhere, "Not at all. I stopped to shower."

I am still laughing at him as we take the elevator down to the lower level. In the lower level he looks at the vehicles and then me, "How do you feel about riding one of the bikes with me?"

My heart races as I tell him, "Really? We could?" He nods and I say, "Yes! I would love that!"

Moments later we are racing through the tunnels. The wind whipping by and the feel of the bike between my legs as I hold tightly to Chance. This is exactly as amazing as I thought it would be. All too soon we are at the main castle and Chance says, "Maybe don't tell my brothers I brought you on the bike?"

My smile slips a little, "Am I not allowed to ride the bikes?"

He shakes his head, "No, it is more that I wasn't supposed to drive the way I normally would with you on the back. But you seemed so happy, and like you were enjoying it as much as I do. I just kept going faster to see when you would be uncomfortable but you never were."

"Of course not! It was amazing. Your brothers are entirely too protective. I love it. And more importantly, they need to remember more consistently that I am my own person. Capable of making my own decisions. However, I won't say anything because I don't want them to give you any shit about it. Now let's go see if your brothers are feeling reasonable today."

We find Knox and Malic in Knox's office. They are thrilled to see me in the castle again. After hugs and scorching hot kisses, Malic is the one that asks, "What happened to bring you home?"

"My father's diaries. It's time for me to go get them."

Knox's eyes flick toward Malic before he says, "Perhaps we could go next week?"

Malic rushes to agree, "Yes, we really are quite busy the rest of this week."

Narrowing my eyes I look hard at each of them. Chance settles into a chair, chuckling. I smell Gage in the hall but I refuse to acknowledge him right now.

"Knox, Malic, I need you both to pay really close attention to what I am saying right now. I am humoring your overprotective nonsense with letting you know that I am going there. With giving you the opportunity to come along so you can feel like you are protecting me. In reality," I wave a hand toward the wall behind me, creating a portal directly in front of my house, "I can go at any time I please. I could have gone this morning while Chance was training and you two were here."

Knox rubs the bridge of his nose, "When you put it that way, I suppose we do need to be more accommodating and less overprotective."

Malic looks over my shoulder toward the door and smiles, "But we insist that Gage come with us. For safety."

Glaring at him I say, "Fine, but it's on you if he kills me."

I hear Gage say, "I can assure you Valdís, I have no desire to kill you."

His voice is deep and low, it sends a frisson of pleasure through me. Swallowing around the sudden lump in my throat I tell him, "Good. Hekate would be pissed if you actually succeeded." He chuckles and I shake my head to clear it. "When will you be ready to leave?"

Somehow it doesn't take them long to collect themselves and minutes later we are in a vehicle and on our way. Gage and Chance are seated across from me. Gage is watching me. His eyes are steady and intense, the combination is odd and yet, enticing. No! We are not repairing another man. He is going to have to sort himself. And convince me. Nicely dammit. All too soon I see my house come into view. My stomach is suddenly doing flips and I can't help but hope that Eirene is somewhere else. The car stops and my kings exit the vehicle first, Knox reaching back in to take my hand and help me out of the vehicle. Taking a deep breath I look up at the house. I don't know if I miss it or I just feel like I should. It doesn't matter right now. Right now I just have to get across this yard to the barn and collect my father's diaries. With one last look at the house I lead the way across the yard toward the barn.

We are halfway there when my kings surround me and two of Eirene's guards come running over. "What are you doing? You can't just wander around here!"

"Excuse you? This is my house. Just because I am at the castle right now doesn't make it any less my home."

The one on the left blusters, "We still need to inform Eumeleia!"

Tipping my head to one side a bit I ask him, "Why Eumeleia? Where is Eirene? And why is it inform Eumie? Where is she? Why didn't she come out with you? Why didn't Eirene come out to flap around and be mad?"

The guards appear reluctant to answer but the one on the right finally says, "We don't know where Lady Eirene is and Eumeleia is at her husband Pelos' home."

Gage takes the opportunity to say, "What a shame. Now would have been as good a time as any to arrest her for treason."

The guards pale and quickly excuse themselves to go back in the house, leaving us to continue on. The barn is quiet and empty when we enter. I look at the stalls that once housed mine and my father's horses. I can only hope that Eirene sold them. She is spiteful enough to have had them murdered just to get at me. Sold. She sold them and that is what I am going to choose to believe until proven otherwise.

My father's office is in the back right corner of the barn. He always said he preferred it there because no one could sneak up on him. Turning the knob I push the door lightly, letting it swing open on well oiled hinges as I touch the switch for the light. The office looks exactly as my father left it other than the bones. The bones laid out so carefully on the floor. The bones of our horses. Oh lady, I feel the bile rising and I just make it to a bucket before my stomach empties everything I had for the past two days. Someone pulls my hair back from my face and holds it, rubbing my back between my shoulders as I try to get the image out of my head. I hate her so much.

My stomach stops roiling and I lean back against the wall, keeping my eyes shut. Someone presses a cool, damp cloth to my forehead and puts a second one in my hand. I use the second one to wipe my mouth clean. Then I hear

Gage saying, "They've gotten the bones out, you can open your eyes now."

My eyes fly open to see Gage standing directly in front of me. Gage was caring for me? His face isn't hungry looking like it was the first time I saw him. His scent has been all around me all this time and I am so used to being insanely turned on anymore that I can still think clearly, and see that he is completely clear-headed. He is actually focused on caring for me.

He asks, "Are you ready to collect your father's diaries?"

"I think maybe I am. Thank you for taking care of me."

He nods, his lips quirking up on one side in a half smile. I pat his arm once and he says, "Careful, little witch. you'll start something you aren't quite ready to finish."

My breath catches and for just a moment I wonder, but now isn't the time so I offer a small smile as I go back toward my father's office. Thankfully it is free of anything... anything that shouldn't be there. Stopping at the door I put my feet together, heels at the opening of the door. Taking careful steps I walk five steps into the room, stopping and carefully turning on my left heel without lifting it. Right foot lined up next to the left again, I lift my left and take seven more steps. Stopping again I keep my left foot in place as I bring my right knee to the ground. Pressing my thumb to the end of my toes I extend my first finger as far as I can and press it gently on the floor. A barely heard click and a large square piece of the floor lowers before sliding into a pocket revealing a trove of books. There must be at least fifty thick journals under here, every one with the spine labeled in a span of years. Knox says, "Your father wrote a lot."

Malic walks around to the other side of the opening, "Let's get these and get out of here. This place makes my skin itchy."

I nod in agreement, I don't want to stay here either. Not even the ghost of my father is here in these walls. But the journals before me, they might just give me a little window into his life. A few answers about my past and his. "Let's," my voice cracks and I clear my throat, "um, let's get these out of here."

Knox and Malic each grab an armful of books and head for the vehicle. They are back fast and I know they are using their speed to keep me from walking back and forth. It's sweet. Mildly annoying but I get the why of it. Chance and Gage aren't pretending at all. The two of them are leaning against either side of the door, very obviously guarding. I suppose it isn't the worst thing ever. The kings have the books in the vehicle quickly, I press the button once more and the door slides back into place, silent as the day it was installed.

My kings surround me as we exit the barn. we all stop when Flaviana comes running out the front door of the house. She runs directly to me, "Take me with you! Please don't leave me here! I haven't anywhere else to go, no family. And I just can't stay here any longer. Please," her face is blotchy and red, "don't make me stay in this place."

"Let me see your ears first." She looks at me like I am insane but, I know that if she has the mark of the Outsiders she won't be allowed anywhere in the castle. A quick check and I find only bare skin. "Ok, I don't see any reason for you to stay here. Do you need to get anything from inside?"

Flaviana shakes her head no, "I just need my bag from the bushes by the fence. I was going to leave tonight."

"Well. Let's go then. You can stay in the Witches Keep."

Valdís

The first volume I start looking through was started shortly after my father had been poisoned. He talks about the poisoning and how he figured out it was Eirene. It gets more interesting when his research brings him to the realization that Eirene isn't just an Outsider. That Eirene is a descendant of the ones sent here to kill the kings. And possibly royalty? The journal doesn't say what research or how he found out, but it does refer to things that happened the year I was born.

Setting this one down I pull out the one that starts before I was born and ends a year or so after. It begins with the troubles of a young couple trying to get pregnant. My father and Eirene had been trying to get with child for many years before I was born and it had begun to wear on my father. He had gone to be tested many times, but Eirene always balked at the testing. He forced her to get testing done. He told her that he believed she was hiding something with her refusal to get testing done. She reluctantly went with him and had it done. When the results came in and the office called them back in, it was to tell them that they would never have a child together because Eirene is an Outsider.

My father almost left her over that. He did leave her at the doctor's office after they fought right there because she had been hiding this information from him since they met, including keeping the mark covered.

It was a week later when she arrived at his house in tears and begging for another chance, he was swayed. He wrote that he didn't know why but he felt like it was something he had to do. And that is when the dreams began. Eirene was talking about having a child implanted in her. Begging my father to work with her so she doesn't lose face before the other women of her status. Meanwhile, my father is having terrible dreams about monsters springing from Eirene's womb. Hearing voices in the dreams screaming as the monsters devoured the island.

He refused her over and over till finally she came to him with the idea of a surrogate. And this is how Dagma came to be my mother. His story is similar to hers, just more about how he and Eirene fought until he finally consented to ask.

But the dreams didn't stop. They changed. Suddenly his dreams are of time and keys and warring deities, a lineage that stretches back to Hekate herself. And a mission unfinished.

I need to talk to her.

Malic

This is the first time she has been back in her room since she went to stay at the keep. Epaphras took over caring for Flaviana as soon as we got back to the castle. Some of the guards helped us to carry all of the journals up to Valdís' room after she tells us that is where she would like to read them.

All four of us went with her, staying as she reads through the journals. Gage sat away from everyone, his eyes only on her. We sit with her for hours as she reads and during certain passages, cries. The one she chose to read first included the time period around when her father was poisoned and, if I have the timing right, the year she was born.

Her eyes are bright with tears and the tracks of them have yet to dry on her cheeks when she closes the journal after reading the final page. She stares blindly at the journal for long moments before she sits up straight and puts here feet on the floor, "Hekate, I need answers."

We all watch in amazement as she appears. Her dark eyes take in all the journals around Valdís along with the one still in her lap. She looks Valdís in the eye, "I suppose I can't avoid it any longer."

Valdís says, "I think I need to know at this point."

Hekate calls in her own chair and seats herself. A steaming cup appears in her hand and the match to it appears on the table before Valdís. After taking a sip Hekate says, "Somehow tea has always made hard discussions a little more bearable. Let's start at the beginning, shall we? A very long time ago, before anyone in this room was even a possibility in their ancestors loins, I took a human lover. It was entirely against the rules but he was kind and good in a way that doesn't come along very often. I fell in love with him and knowing that he would eventually die and be taken from me, I enjoyed the time we would have, making sure that he was happy for the entirety of his life. I granted him everything he ever wanted, including a single child. The child was a daughter, and so began the line that would one day lead to your birth. Your father reminded me of him in many ways. All that could have just been how things went only, gods and goddesses are the same as humans with more power and knowledge. That knowledge doesn't always make us smarter.

We are often just as capricious, envious, and ignorant as humans can be. We just have more capacity to destroy or create along with limitless time to do so. We also have torrid love affairs. Some of us are shitty and like to think everything in the universe is their due.

Once upon a time I was... younger and less experienced. My power was not fully realized and my mind had not the emotional information needed to read others of my kind. I entered into a relationship with the god of the Outsiders. I won't say his name, because he is always listening for it."

Valdís says, "This whole war is a really bad breakup? A crazy ex that just won't leave you alone?"

Hekate sighs, "Well, I suppose it could be summed up that way, yes."

Valdís's face falls, "There isn't any way that he will let this go is there? A lot more people are going to die over this, aren't they?"

I watch Hekate nod, "They will. All for his love of power. I left him when I realized that he wanted me for the power I possess. He tried to force me to give my power to him. After he tried to siphon it from me. Unfortunately for him, my mother was keen and crafty and wise. She had taught me things that prevented him doing that. It was after I left him that I fell in love with the mortal. I kept us hidden while he was alive and I trained my daughter in all the things she would need to know and do being between the worlds as she is."

Valdís holds up a hand, "You said is. Is your daughter still alive?"

"She is. She spends less time in this dimension than I do, in part because the god of the Outsiders would love to possess her. She is with my mother."

Valdís nods, "Of course he would be like that."

"Indeed. She did live here on the big island for a long time. She is the reason I blessed my people with much longer than usual life spans. I wanted her happiness to last as long as possible. She had many children and her mate had a long, happy life with her. But eventually, the God of the Outsiders figured out who she is and how she is connected to me. That is when he came to this land and tried to take her. He didn't know then how powerful she is. She sent her children running to the forest and calling me while she worked at burning him crispy. When I got there he was more than a little crisp and my daughter was furious. The fire had burnt up every last painting she had ever done of her beloved mate. The house she had shared with him, all of it was nothing but ashes. I sent the God of the Outsiders into the middle of the ocean, hoping that the salt in his wounds would burn more. It did and he was incensed about the whole thing. When he finally fished himself out of the ocean and tried to come back here, he found that I had blessed this land and for him to set any part of himself on it caused his flesh to burn again in a most unpleasant manner."

Valdís sighs, "But he managed to keep some of his people secreted here on the island."

Hekate sips her tea, seeming lost in thought. "He did, but that was not entirely his doing. He didn't get the same sort of power that I was gifted with. Which means that what I have passed on to you is power that he hasn't got. And he can't peer through the mists of time. I saw that there was a way that he could take my power from me. The results would not be what he imagined. We, all of us have our weaknesses. Mine is that power shared multiplies. Sounds like a fine thing, possibly even a good thing. But in my case, it is not. The more people that share in my power, because all of you share in my power, the stronger I become. There was a thread to the future, it showed him gifting my power to his people so that he could feed from their power. And I became something else. Something terrible that had to be eliminated by my mother and daughter. I do not wish to cause them that pain." She shakes her head as if clearing away things best left alone, "That is why I limited my people's ability to procreate, in order to keep the number of people with my power small. But you Valdís, you are a different thing all together. When I saw how he could take my power I hid that key in space and time. In you Valdís. You are the key to all of my power."

"Me? What? Oh no, why would you trust me with that? I'm no one. I've nearly died so many times and--"

"Silence! You are exactly where the key must stay. You are so much more than you believe yourself to be. The way things have happened is the only path that leads to success. I cannot see everything on this path. I am able to see small pieces leading in the direction that keeps me from becoming the bane of this dimension and many others. You are the key to all of this. That much I have seen. While all the witches are part of my line, you are the only one with an unbroken lineage. A direct descendant of my daughter and myself. Technically, a descendant on both sides of your family, but it is your father's side that is directly descended from me. That is why you are so much more powerful than any other witch."

Valdís sighs, "And still a rather half-assed witch."

"Not half-assed, kind. Your heart is the best part of you. That is why instead of leveling a field full of people you spoke my name, only temporarily incapacitating people. You and I both know you could have left that field full of char and lost souls. Once upon a time I would have. You could, but you won't if you have any other option. Even an option that includes harm to you. You are selfless in ways that most of us choose not to be. That is why the key to my power must rest in you until... until things are settled."

~

Gage

Valdís looks dazed. Hekate hugs her and moves away, going to Malic. She taps his face lightly, reminding him that dashing off with half thought out plans will always lead to disaster. She says, "You must use your mind if you are going to keep her alive. Rise above your fears." She turns to Knox, "You are on the right track. A council of witches is just what this land needs. Make it strong." She walks over to Chance and takes his face in her hands, "It's going to hurt like hell. You'll live through it and your actions will keep her alive. You stick to her, don't leave her side for anything. We are all counting on you. I know you won't fail us or her."

Then she turns to find me in the corner, I stand as she walks to me. She stops before me, "My dear, of course she is frightened of you. You are half feral. Show her that you are more than that. Show her that feral creatures can choose people too. You'll have to let her in if you want her to accept you." I nod and she leans in, hugging me. I carefully hug her back and release her quickly. She chuckles, "You'll probably need to let her hug you too."

Nine

EIRENE

My guards and I are on the shore when the boat arrives. It seems to come from out of nowhere. Appearing in the harbor as if by magic. I watch the men, all dressed in form-fitting, dark clothing, as they get into a smaller boat. The boat is lowered into the water and an engine starts almost immediately. The boat zips across the waves, making it to the shoreline in minutes. All but one man exits the boat, the one that stays takes the small boat back across the water.

The men turn and walk across the beach to me, stopping to kneel before me, "Your majesty, it is an honor."

The joy it gives me to hear that in reference to myself has no end. I feel lit up from the inside. "Rise, we should get off this beach, it is not entirely safe for me to be out in the open."

The men rise smoothly and surround me, leaving my

guards to lead the way back to the house. Back in the house we talk about what they have been instructed to do and the timeline we will have once they start the mission.

They are going to collect Valdís and put her on the boat. Her being the key makes her useful and necessary for my God. But it means that once we get her, we have to leave fast. The plans for that are pretty clear but then I remember my prisoners. He said I need to bring them. "I have some prisoners here, Lords of this land. Our God said that we must bring them too. How shall we work this?"

The one that seems to be the lead of the group, Harris says, "Why not get them loaded now? If we just put them on the boat now, they can wait there until we are finished here and we won't have to concern ourselves with getting them there quickly."

"Perfect."

∼

Ingemar

I am incredibly relieved to hear that we are going to be taken to the boat soon. I know that the chances of us being killed are, for now, a lot lower. Between getting away from the kings that definitely want us dead now and the fact that her God wants us alive and brought with them, it buys us a little more time.

Chances are we will never see our homeland again. Perhaps I can leverage things and convince Eirene to keep me alive. I have obviously underestimated her, and fuck if that isn't galling.

I was certain that she would be nothing more than a pawn in my bid to become king. It would appear I was wrong about who is the pawn in this game.

Pelos

The feeling in my chest is so unfamiliar that it took me some time to realize exactly what it is. And still, even after realizing that I am happy, it has taken some adjustment on my part. I have lashed out at my sweet Eumeleia. She didn't deserve any of the harsh things I said that hurt her feelings. And for some reason, she forgave me. She is kind to me and patient, talking to me as an equal.

But the time we have spent together has revealed that I am no where near to being her equal.

She praises me and I want more than anything to be worthy of her praise. I know that the person my father prefers me to be is not someone that is worthy of Eumeleia's love. And there is the problem. If my father can come home and take over the running of this house again, I won't have any choice but to at least appear to behave the way he wants. I can't do that to her.

I can't let my father treat her the way he treated my mother. I have to protect her. I don't want to disappoint her the way I know I will if my father shows up here to take over, because I will certainly murder him where he stands the first time he looks in her direction.

My decision made, I seek out my Eumeleia. I find her in the kitchen, working on the menu with our cook. Even cook seems enchanted by her. She smiles when she sees me, I don't deserve her. But I will.

"Eumeleia, my love, would you come speak with me in private?"

"Of course, excuse me. I will return to check the preparations for tonight's meal. I am sure it will be excellent."

"Yes ma'am, thank you."

She slips her arm in mine as she draws even with me. "Where shall we speak my Pelos?"

I never thought I would enjoy hearing my name spoken so very much. "I thought perhaps we could speak in my father's office."

Her face falls a bit, but I think she will be pleased as we talk through my ideas. Inside the office I move a chair around the desk so that she and I can sit together on the same side of the desk. She looks pleased by this as she sits, "What is it you want to discuss?"

"I have been thinking about my father and your mother and their plans. I think we should distance ourselves from everything they were, are, and all that they have ever represented. I can't speak for your mother, but my father was never what anyone would term a good person. His life has been lived with only his comfort in mind. I mean, he killed my mother."

"Oh Pelos, my mother is really no better. She definitely killed my father. I feel certain that had she been able to pull it off, she would have happily killed Valdís. I think she came quite close to it at times. I remember one odd morning where the family woke up to Valdís missing. When she was found she was on the beach, supposedly with no memory of how she arrived there."

"It would seem that our parents are both quite awful. And that is why I feel we should let go of everything they were striving for. You don't want to be a queen, I have no interest in my father or myself being king. I want us to send a letter to the kings, apologizing for our parents actions. You collect everything of yours from your family home and let it go to Valdís if she wants it. I mean, that was what started all of this, right? She was trying to keep the inheritance your mother was determined to wrest from her."

"Yes, that is most of it. I confess, I think she cared less about the estate and more about the people. My father's way of tending to them and my mother's way of handling them were very different. My father was concerned with their welfare while my mother was, well, more concerned with her comfort."

"And that is more reason for us to let it go. We don't need it. I want us to keep my family home. Both of us denounce our parents, we request that my father be removed from the line of succession, we be granted the holding of this estate and allowed to carry on with our lives and without the fear of my father legally being allowed to tear it all away from us."

"Oh Pelos, I love it. But should we wait? We don't even know what happened to our parents. Perhaps we should send a letter denouncing our parents actions, but wait until we know what happened to them before we go further?"

"My love, we open ourselves to many troubles with

waiting. I ask that you trust me. I know my father. He is alive and in hiding somewhere. Biding his time and waiting to return. He is more terrible than you can imagine and you would not be safe with him in the same house as you. I fear... I fear that I would shame myself by murdering him for even looking in your direction. Will you trust me to put our family first? Will you work with me on this? Please, Eumeleia, I really feel we must do this for our future."

Watching her face while she ponders my words, I worry that she will not allow it. That she won't take the danger my father presents seriously. Then she says, "I trust you Pelos. If you believe we need to protect ourselves, then that is what we will do."

Relief pours through my body, easing a tension I didn't realize I was holding. "Thank the Goddess! Let's compose the letter now. The sooner this is done, the better. We will collect your things this afternoon."

Ten

Valdís

The shields these women are creating are fantastic. I had Bettina create a shield over top a bush here in the courtyard. Now we are all inspecting it after I have shot at it three different times. I hit it with fire, ice, and rocks. The shield has held up well. I look at Bettina, "How do you feel? Is it hard to continue holding it? Did it strain you when I was firing at it?"

She sighs, "It is harder to hold it when you are firing at it. But, your magic is different? When the others fire at it, I am more easily able to hold it. You magic almost seems to pluck at the shield? Like it would take it apart if you kept firing at it."

"Oh. Maybe I shouldn't be the one to take aim at your creations then?"

Bettina shakes her head, "I think you should. No one else challenges me the way you do. I think that I could maybe figure out a way to tie this off, so that I am not supporting it. It wouldn't be as strong but it would free me to do other things, like fire back. I found out that I can shoot through my shields without destroying them."

"That is good! Can you do that while you hold it or only if you have it tied off?"

"So far, I've only tried it without any active stress. Holding it over myself and firing at a target. I think maybe with practice I could hold the shield and fire. I just am not there yet."

"You are doing amazing! We should all celebrate how far we all have come with this. We have gone from having no magic at all to pushing our magic to the limits and doing new things with it.," I turn to look around and raise my voice so all can hear me, "Every one of you is doing so well! I am really proud of the work you have done in your craft, to improve your abilities in utilizing your magic. You should all be proud of yourselves." The women raise a cheer and I give them a few moments before I say, "Now, let's save some more witches, who wants to talk to the women and who wants to hold shields for the ones doing the talking?"

The women start organizing things, and I look to my left as I feel eyes on me. Gage is watching me from his perch under a tree. I am conflicted about him. He was terrifying the first day I met him. Today he is my guard because his brothers all have other things to do. Or so they say. To be honest though, I haven't been as frightened of him since that day at my house. Now, as he watches me, his presence is oddly comforting.

"Valdís?"

I look up, realizing they have been trying to get my attention. "Oh! Are we ready for the portal?"

One of the women says yes and I watch as shields go over two other women and another shows me the image of the place I need to open a portal in. A little focus and one spell later, the portal is opened. I watch as the two women go through the portal. They find the woman quickly but come back without her. We all feel the lingering sadness as the portal closes on a woman convinced she is evil for having a power that the men cannot hold. The next two portals are happier. Two more witches come home and we are done collecting women for the day.

Gage

My brothers are doing what they can to encourage her to not be afraid of me. Including today's pretense of all three of them having something else to do. I know very well that they aren't all so busy that one of them couldn't be here. I appreciate the gesture though.

Valdís is fully in her element here, helping these women train, she is magnificent to watch. She is kind and understanding with each of them, working with them till they achieve their goals. She feels my eyes on her and turns to stare back, a slight frown on her face. There isn't a trace of fear in her scent though. She smiles a little in my direction, could she actually be smiling about me? Then the others call her name and she is focused on them once again.

Dagma has been watching me all morning and now she is heading my way. She seats herself near me, "She will come around. You just keep earning her trust."

I look her way with a frown before turning my gaze back onto Valdís, "What makes you so sure?"

"Well, the other kings behaved a lot worse and they still managed to gain her trust. They don't even have the wolf thing going for them the way you do."

That got my full attention. "What do you mean?"

She purses her lips and rolls her eyes, "I am the resident healer. The best and most powerful healer we have. Since I had to fly blind with healing my son and his beloved I have made it a practice to study the way everyone is put together. How all the parts work with each other. The people that are from this land function in one way, even the ones that came back from the land of the Outsiders. Though admittedly, there are quite a few processes that move slower now that they have been here a minute." She sighs, "Those that are Outsiders, their bodies operate differently. The other kings, things operate slower, almost imperceptibly, but other than that they are exactly the same as people from this land. Then there's you."

Oh no. All this time no one has figured out my secret. Now this healer that happens to be Valdís's mother, of course she would be the one to figure it out.

"And what do you see about me?"

"Well, it took me a little while to figure it out. On the surface you appear to be just like the other kings. Except for these little... almost like storage units. And inside those storage units is all wolf. Which puzzled me a lot. Because how could a human have wolf stored in them? I went through a lot of really exotic ideas at first. But then I remembered a story my grandmother told me. A story she said had been passed down since before there were kings. A story about a certain portion of the population that was not restricted to only one form."

Ah fuck. "And what are you going to do with this information? Now that you know what I am."

"I thought I would offer advice and ask questions until you snarl at me."

A chuckle bubbles up and out of me before I can stop it, "What is the advice?"

"Get her talking to you and listen. She loves dogs, maybe try hanging out with her as a wolf, which she would find much less threatening than the man."

"And what happens when my brothers try to kill me? I think they will not be pleased with the idea of an unknown wolf around Valdís."

"Hm, I wasn't aware that your brothers didn't know. Why keep it secret so long?"

"There just never seemed to be a good time to tell them. My tribe had always kept it secret. We thought no one knew. Then we fought the monster, got made kings, and we had to figure out ways to work together. All while figuring out how to work with being vampires."

"I can see how that would be a little much. There's no

time like now. You could tell them. I think it would likely explain a great many things for them and they would likely go along with the idea of you being around her as a wolf."

"I'll think about it. I don't know if I am ready for that."

"I won't be telling them."

Eleven

EIRENE

He has been studying maps for hours now. I can't take it anymore and I ask, "Why haven't you gone to get her yet?"

"We are trying to keep the operation quiet. In case you ever need to come back here and take up the life you were leading. As well as to avoid an all out war back to the ship."

"I have no intentions of coming back to this place. I would rather run for the ship across the water than continue to wait here. How can we move this along? Is there a way that I can help?"

"Yes. Tell me about this map. Tell me about the places marked here. Are there actual castles here? Is that what this means? Where is Valdís spending most of her time?"

"Ah, I can help with that. Yes, there are real castles here. This one in the middle is where the kings live most of the time. At least when they are here." Moving closer to the table I point at a castle not far from here on the northern end of the island. "Local gossip says the witches are holing up there. She is the lead witch from what I hear, perhaps she is also spending her time there?"

"It would be really convenient if she is. I'll have my men go scout the place tonight. If your information is correct, we may have this done a lot faster than I thought possible."

"Excellent. When do we load the lords onto the ship?"

Valdís

I miss my kings. Gage has been coming to take over guard duty during the day lately. My kings think I have not figured out why they suddenly have so much to do. I realize very well what they are doing and if I am honest, it is working. I find him much less frightening these days and I want to go home. I want my giant bed and sleeping in a cuddled heap with my kings. I think tonight I will go home. I'll brave having Gage take me back to the castle tonight. I turn to see Chance coming out of the bathroom, freshly showered and a towel slung low on his hips. He chuckles and I remember I was going to say something but that towel... He says, "My eyes are up here."

My face heats and I say, "Yes, but that towel is incredibly distracting." I look back out the doors to the balcony and I hear his clothes rustling as he puts them on, "I was thinking that tonight I want to go back to my room."

He joins me as I step out onto the balcony, "Ready to go home, eh? Finding Gage a little less frightening?"

Laughing I say, "Yes, the evil plan hatched by you, Knox, and Malic has indeed worked. He feels much less a threat now that he has been around a bit more. I think watching him and Dagma talking might have helped to sway me." I look out at the view from his balcony. I can't see the other castle from here but I know it is there. "Even if this room has a gorgeous view. I miss seeing all of you more than I have lately."

Chance slips an arm around me, "We miss you too."

I lean into the warmth of him as we enjoy the morning view. Chance tenses suddenly and snatches me back into the room. We are halfway across the room when men land on the balcony. I fire off two shots of ice, knocking the men off their feet. "Chance, stop! We can fight them."

He releases me as more men drop onto the balcony. He darts forward, hitting two of them and sending them flying over the railing. Another swings down, planting his feet in Chance's gut and sending him flying back. With Chance out of the way I start hitting them with ice, large chunks aimed for their heads. Another man swings down and Chance is flying at him as I hit one trying to stand with a large ball of ice that shatters as it hits his forehead. The man that swung down throws something at me, I turn, trying to dodge it and feel something sharp prick my arm. My body goes numb and I fall to the ground. More men swing down and one has something in his hand that hits Chance with projectiles multiple times. It's loud and my Chance is bleeding. The men ignore him as he lays there, coming instead to lift me and strap me onto someone. Every fiber of my being is struggling to move, to do something. Anything. The last thing I see as the man I am strapped to throws himself and me away from the building is my Chance reaching for me.

Gage

My hackles have been up all morning and I don't know why. I was up long before the first rays of the sun waiting for it to be time to go to her. Trying not to frighten her and lose the progress I made with her. The sun is up. It isn't time yet but I can't take it any longer. Grabbing a bike in the garage I take the tunnel to the Witches Keep at speeds that are reckless even for me.

As soon as I reach the top level of the garage there, I know. I smell the Outsiders and the blood. I take off running, shouting to alert the castle. The guards follow me as I head for her room. I've never been inside it but there is no mistaking which one it is. Her scent is overpowering in there, in the hall leading to it. Except today, today it smells of of Outsiders, and the blood of my brother.

I am not surprised when I see Chance bloody on the floor, I am surprised when he moves. Rushing to his side, I kneel beside him. He opens his eyes, "They took her. But she is alive."

He stops to cough blood and I say, "Are you too injured to heal?"

"No. I--"

"Good. I'll go after her--"

"Wait. Get Dagma. She can heal me now. I'll go with you. They are well armed with guns. You need a second."

I hate the time this will take from going after her. "Ok. She'll be here in a moment." I run through the castle, using my nose to find Dagma. When I do find her at breakfast I only tell her, "Chance is hurt." Then I scoop her up and run with her, getting her back to the room faster than I found her. She isn't happy about the speed, and less happy when she realizes where we are and what must have happened. She kneels next to Chance and puts her hands over his chest. She pulls out ten bullets and heals my brother fully within moments. While she heals him I message Knox and Malic.

They have her. Get to the Keep now.

Chance thanks her as he stands. She simply says, "Go get my girl back."

He walks over to the balcony and grabs one of the ropes hanging there, I am there and following him down on another rope before he gets his feet on the castle again. It tears up our hands, and they'll be slow to heal as we run. But everything will speed up when we start ripping out throats.

Twelve

KNOX

My heart froze in my chest when I read the message. I can't breathe as time stops and my whole world is narrowed to that message. Time kicks in again and seems to be moving at twice the speed as I tell Epaphras to get to the Keep now. I take off to the garage, nearly colliding with Malic heading for the same place from a different direction.

And age or three later we are at the keep and running to Valdís's room. Dagma and Bettina are there, along with various guards, some bodies, and a lot of blood. I smell that some of it is Chance's, but not Valdís's. They took her alive. I don't know if I should be happy about that considering what they want to do to her. I look to Dagma, "What happened?"

She turns from staring out the balcony, "I'm not sure. Gage brought me to heal Chance and he didn't explain much before they left. Out the balcony that already had ropes hanging over it. I can only assume those are from the people that took her." She pulls out a handful of bullets, "They must tell some interesting tales about you in the lands of the Outsiders."

I look at her, my brows drawing in, "What do you mean?"

She stretches the hand holding the bullets out, "Can't you smell it? They loaded these things up with garlic and something odd that glows."

Malic snorts, "Fucking idiots. We are not those creatures, but it's just as well if they think we are. Yes, Dagma, they do tell some very odd stories in the Outsider lands."

Looking at Malic I say, "They probably aren't getting her back before they get her off the island."

He shakes his head, "No, they aren't."

I nod, "I'm putting together a council really quick. I have people in mind. Can you handle the travel plans?"

He nods and Dagma speaks up, "I'm going."

We both turn to her, "What?"

She repeats, "I'm going. I am going with you to collect my daughter from these fucking bastards that are so damn determined to have her. I have some very useful skill sets for this and a deep desire to use them. I am coming with you."

Before we can tell her no, Bettina jumps in, "So am I. I know the places you will be searching for her in. I know the damn organization that is after all the witches and Valdís in particular. And my shield work is better than anyone else here."

I look over to Malic and shrug. It would take more time

to argue them out of this than to let them go and they might help. He nods and strides out of the room, phone going to his ear.

"Fine. Help me find Quorin. Someone has to run this place while we are gone and I was going to ask her anyway."

Dagma and Bettina near run out the door, leading the way to Quorin as I follow. The panic over Valdís is still there but I am feeling a little less unhinged for working toward getting her back.

Quorin and the two K's are in the courtyard practicing. Seeing the two K's, I know they have to be on the council. They are shrewd and less fragile than they look. They all seem surprised to see us until Dagma tells them about the kidnapping. Quorin looks to me, "How can we help?"

"You can be the heads of the new ruling council."

Her jaw drops, "I'm sorry, I don't think I heard you correctly. You didn't just--"

Katerine cuts her off, "Yes he did. He didn't mumble either. Tell us more."

I like the two K's so damn much. "I have been working to create the laws that would create a peaceful transfer of power to a ruling council of witches. The document isn't fully ready, but it is close enough and with the entire castle guard backing you alongside Epaphras, you shouldn't have too many problems. And, we will be back as soon as possible to complete the transfer. We would still be available to back up the council as needed. It will start with you three. You will need to add to it, making it a total of thirteen witches. Everyone on the council must be a witch, that is the only real stipulation. If they aren't a witch they aren't on the council."

Quorin nods, "Very well. Dagma, what about you, will you be part of the council?"

She shakes her head no. "I am going to help bring my daughter back. One way or another."

Quorin and the two K's pale at that, Katerine taking Dagma's hand and saying, "You do what you must and don't you count not a one as a mark on your tally. Hekate certainly isn't going to mark it against you for whatever you need to do to get her back."

Dagma nods, her face grim. Now I wonder just what she is planning to do that makes them all so serious. Shaking it off I tell them, "Come, Epaphras is bound to be here by now. Let's get as much sorted as we can before I have to leave."

Thirteen

CHANCE

Rappelling down the castle wall was faster, if more painful. My hands are torn and bloodied to the bone. I suspect that Gage's are just as bad. We take off running, following the tracks of the men that took her. They have a long head start on us, but we are faster.

Minutes later we see them, moving at a steady pace. They aren't even looking back. We grab one each from the back of the pack, the other men start shooting in our direction as they run when the men we snatched scream. Their screams don't last long. Ripping the shirt of the man I snatched up away from his neck, I hold his body in front of me as a shield while I feed. A couple bullets make it through but with the fresh blood it doesn't matter. My body has pushed them out even before I finish feeding. Dropping the body I start running for the others. I pass Gage as he stops to rip the head off another, the spray of blood doesn't slow me and I grab another. His screams are shrill as I snatch his arms from his body. I start to toss him off to the side but the fucker bites me and I snatch his head from his body. What the hell? They don't even feed like we do.

Fucking weirdo. I hope this doesn't get infected. How was it that Malic got that infection? I don't remember, I need to check. Later. I realize as I run to catch up that we are practically at the coast and I can see a small boat waiting to take off. Gage grabs another guy. Fuck this is time consuming. But we can't leave them able to possibly attack us from behind. I grab another and rip his throat out even as I see the other two dive into the boat with Valdís.

The guy waiting in the boat guns the engine as they land. Dammit. Gage runs into the water a bit before he realizes that we aren't made for speed in the water. He wades back to shore as I pull out my phone. A few taps on the screen and I wait as the line connects.

Malic answers, "Did you get her?"

"No. We got most of them though."

"Too much head start. I'll have the boat ready shortly."

Quorin

"So you and King Knox have been working on this for a while?"

Epaphras nods, "Yes. The king is quite certain that it

should be witches running this country, not, how did you put it? A bunch of kings that never wanted to rule a household, much less a whole damn country."

"I guess that's a way of looking at it. King Knox, you said that it should be thirteen? Is there a reason why?"

"If I had to guess, he is probably playing on the strange ideas the Outsiders have about witches needing a coven of thirteen to be effective."

Kalina laughs, "Well they haven't been paying attention have they? My Dagma can kill a man where he stands, she just doesn't want to most of the time."

Epaphras pales, "Is that so? Remind me not to get on her bad side."

Katerine laughs darkly, "You're safe. She'll get her fill for a long time to come today while she is out with the kings getting our girl back."

A shiver runs down my spine. I think maybe I don't want to be on Dagma's bad side either. "Do any of you have opinions on what other witches we should put on the council?"

King Knox says, "Only that they be witches and it would be better if they felt like this land is their home. I think it would not serve anyone very well for parts of the council to be wishing to be elsewhere. You can introduce us all when we get back. The council will be in charge at least until will get back," he looks toward the door, "and likely for much longer with a possible pause for an official transfer."

Epaphras nods, "Sire, I think you can go. We can certainly take care of the rest."

King Knox's face lights up, "You can? That would be great, really. I know my brothers are trying to wait for me. We would all like to get going after her."

He nearly runs out the door as we watch. Epaphras turns back to us, "So, who are we thinking?"

~

Valdís

I feel certain my entire body is going to be nothing but a bruise. I was thrown all about as they ran from the destruction chasing them. The dive into this smaller boat was heart-stopping. I don't know what they got me with but I fucking hate it. I feel like my brain is disconnected from the control center for my body. I can't even close my eyes.

Just lay here and stare at the floor of the boat until they see fit to move me. The sound of the engine slows and then stops. I hear movement around me and then a jolt that shakes the entire boat. I am lifted again and the men start talking, "Fucking hell, we lost most of the damn crew! Those monsters ate most of our crew. They ate them!"

I hear Eirene's voice and my blood runs cold, "Of course they did! I told you they are vampires! What did you think that meant?"

"Well the garlic and UV bullets barely phased them, so what the fuck kind of vampires are they? Some new fuckin' breed that has immunity to those things? It took a lot of bullets to knock the one down and he was still up hunting us as we ran here!"

Oh thank Hekate! Chance lives! I could cry with relief if I had any capability of doing so. I hear Eirene, "Oh look, our little key is crying. Take her below and close her eyes. It's creepy how she's just staring into the sky like that."

Fourteen

Malic

Knox is taking forever to get finished. I just want to go. I want to hunt down those bastards. All of them. Just start picking off everyone that is part of the ruling class of the organization till there is no one left to come after her.

Instead, I am just pacing. Waiting while Knox handles people to run the country. Because it could be days or weeks, depending on how far they get. How fast they can go. How much help they have. How much--

Hekate's words ring through my mind. Half planned things lead to destruction. But I have connections. I can arrange things. I can have people watching the coast. I can do things. I know Knox can hear me from in the room so I tell him, "I'm going to get things ready, I'll see you at the boat."

I take off running, heading for the garage and the bike I rode here.

~

Valdís

Ow! My face hurts. I feel someone slap it and then Eirene says, "Wake up bitch!"

I try to bring my hands up to protect my face but that isn't working. Maybe something small? Maybe if I can open my eyes she will stop slapping me? After a lot of focus and two more slaps, I manage to open my eyes. I opened my eyes! Yes! The stuff they gave me must be wearing off.

I see Eirene's hand lift to slap me again but she notices my eyes open and smiles, "Oh good! You are awake now." She slaps me again anyway, "If I had known how useful you were going to be I certainly wouldn't have wasted all that time trying to get rid of you. Who could have known that you would be the key for me to get back to the real world? The world where I am royalty and there are no damned kings to gainsay me. You are the completion of my family's mission to that stupid island. I just wanted you to know that you, darling stepdaughter, are nothing more than my ticket home. I am going now to the life that I have always deserved. You have given me this gift and I thought you should get to hold on to that little bit of information as you serve my God for the rest of your days, whether you like it or not."

She starts to leave but turns back and slaps me again. I watch her leave the room this time. My face has got to be black and blue with all this. I have to get out of here. My eyelids are under my control again and I can definitely feel every bit of my face. Maybe the rest of me is coming back to me? Closing my eyes to focus I work on trying to wiggle my fingers. I've never in my life had to focus so hard just to move any part of my body. Fuck! This shit has to let go already. Then my finger twitches, it's a small movement, but I can work with it. Long minutes pass as I get my hands working.

But they do start working. I wonder... if I open a portal will it work as we move over the ocean? I have to try it. Maybe I can drag myself through it, if it works.

Since my hands are working, even if my arms are still pretty fucking shaky, I try it. My gestures aren't the sharpest ever but they do the trick and I watch as the portal starts to form. And dissipates before it really opens to anything. Ok then. I guess portals as I move over water are not a thing.

Thunder cracks over the ship and I am thrown off the bunk they had me laying on. Oh, that doesn't feel good. That doesn't feel good at all. Before I can even try to sit up I am thrown up, only to collide with the floor as it rises up to meet me. Fuck, as if I didn't have enough aches. Why is pain the first thing to really return? I get my fingers wrapped around a handle and manage to avoid another collision. What the hell is going on out there?

Fifteen

EIRENE

I am standing at the front of the ship when the storm appears out of nowhere. A wave hits the ship, tossing me toward the railing and I manage to grab on to it, nearly jerking my arms from their sockets but stopping me from falling into a suddenly very rough sea. One of the men comes over and helps me into the cabin, where I am not likely to be washed away into the sea by this crazy weather.

I look around and I realize, this weather is only over us. But I see the land, even as I feel the ship power forward. The seas are calm and sunny not far from our ship. The captain races for the dock in the cove even as the storm intensifies. It's all coming at us so fast, I brace myself for the possible impact, he can't possibly stop it without an impact. Hopefully the little bitch with still be useful if her fool neck breaks in the impact.

I feel the ship slowing dramatically, even as the storm is dropping massive amounts of water, thunder and lightning cracking everywhere. The smallest of bumps tells me we did hit, but not so hard as I thought we would. I hope the man is paid especially well.

Some of the men run in and bundle me up in a rain slick, it's huge and covers most of me. But judging by the way the wind is whipping outside this space, it isn't going to help. I can see people, my people, coming out of buildings. Watching as we are attacked by the weather.

The men hold onto me as we exit the room and head down the walkway they have lowered to meet with the solid gray path that extends out into the water next to the ship. They hustle me to a vehicle and help me in. The storm is so intense I can barely see out the vehicle.

Moments later the vehicle is rocketing forward, the storm staying with us. Their goddess must have figured out that we have her. Well, too damn bad. We are keeping her and we are going to use our little key.

Even as I think that the storm intensifies, hail hitting the vehicle. The windshield is spiderwebbing, cracks spreading as the chunks of ice hit. Loud bangs sound from under the vehicle as it swerves and the ride is horribly jolting now. The man driving shouts over the noise, "Hold on, we're almost there!"

I feel like the vehicle is going to flip as he makes a turn, taking us through a gate into a rather drab looking compound. He hits the brakes and the vehicle keeps sliding for a bit as a wall looms ahead. The vehicle manages to stop before we hit it but it can't be far from having hit it. We sit, listening to the hail batter the vehicle as the other one stops next to us. They have the hail issues but it would appear they got to keep their tires. I move to get out but the man sitting with me shouts, "Wait, it isn't safe yet. We're going to put her out first."

Oh, what a fantastic idea. I sit back and wait as they open a door and start pushing Valdís out before them. The rain doesn't touch her and the hail stops immediately. We all get out of the vehicle now, the men putting me next to Valdís. She is able to walk now, if not well. The lords are following behind us, much more meek than I have ever seen them. It is good for them. We get to the door and I stop them, "Wait, I want her goddess to see this." Drawing my hand back I slap Valdís, staggering her with the force of it. Thunder claps above us and I smile, "We can continue now gentlemen."

KNOX

As soon as she suggests that I can go ahead and leave, I am racing for the garage. My bike is there waiting. Jumping on it I take the tunnels at speeds well beyond what I usually would. Within minutes I am coming to the tunnel exit near the docks. I hit the control button for the door and slow my bike for the ramp. If I go up it at these speeds I will launch myself into the sea. It would take much longer for them to fish me out of the ocean than for me to just slow down and take the ramp like I've driven before. There are a few guards near the dock as I pull up to it, they take my bike, leaving me free to run for the boat. Malic gets the engines going and starts the boat moving slowly back even as I leap across to land lightly on the deck. Once I am on board, Malic guns it and the boat takes off. I lurch with it, but it's fine.

Malic is pushing the boat to go as fast as it can and luckily, it is pretty fast. It won't win any races, but it will get us there pretty fast. Fairly quickly we see a boat in the distance. It is still well ahead of us and moving fast. There is a strange shimmer in the air that we just passed through, I turn to look at it and I see it fade away. I can't see our home anymore. Fuck me, if we had been any slower our boat could have been cut in half. I'm going to try real hard not to think about that. I don't know that we will catch up to them in the water, but at least we won't be as far behind them as we could be had we missed that.

Gage and Chance come to stand next to me, watching the boat we are chasing. As I watch little gold sparkles start flowing out behind the boat, it looks like if Valdís's portal was... she's alive and conscious! No sooner than I think that a storm cloud appears over the boat and starts pounding it. But only on and directly around that boat. Glancing at my brothers I say, "Well, if I had to guess, I would say that is definitely them. If I was a betting man, I would bet that Hekate knows now."

From behind me I hear, "I am aware, yes. And I am not pleased. He knows. He knows that she is the key. He hid his people from me, the bastard. You must keep them from using her to take my power from the other witches. Or just giving the power to other witches. They will be working to use her for the power as soon as they get her on land. I will slow them as much as I can."

We all turned to face her when she started speaking. But Chance is the one that says, "Why would you make that a thing? Seems like a design flaw to me."

She scowls at him, "It isn't something I did, just something I have to deal with. Possibly it didn't occur to the one that created me that any of the others like me would try to steal my power. It seems like a ridiculous thing when you have the amount of power that we have. Why would you need someone else's power?"

Gage, silent all this time, says, "If you have all these different strains of power, what is he good at?"

Hekate looks out over the ocean, "Monsters. He is really good at making monsters."

"He made that thing we fought?"

She nods, "He did. But when that didn't work he changed tactics. He is still making monsters, but they look like people. You can't tell the difference between regular people and his monsters just for looking at them. Now, they look just like everyone else." She gestures toward the shoreline, "They are taking her inland now. I can't stop them without possibly injuring her. She isn't completely recovered from the drug they gave her yet. I will continue to help as I can, but there are rules for even the ones such as me."

Gage

We are at least half an hour behind them. Every moment spent chafes at my control. We slide into mooring smoothly and there are men waiting for us. I am suspicious until Malic yells, "Toss them the lines, they are with us."

We do as he says and getting off the boat goes much faster. One of the men leads the four of us to a parking area, he points at a set of bikes and says, "The keys are in them. Three extra helmets as you requested."

Malic thanks him in cash while the rest of us go to the bikes. Dagma looks at me and pushes Bettina toward the back of Knox's bike. Then the fool woman walks back over and says, "I'm riding there with you." I open my mouth to argue and she holds up a hand, "No. I am riding with you and that's final."

"Fine. But you both understand that we aren't here to take prisoners. We aren't here to try and avoid killing. We are here to rescue her and do so as fast as possible. While taking down their numbers as much as we can without slowing ourselves."

Dagma looks over at the other one, Bettina. They both look back at me and smile as Dagma says, "We are fine with the blood bath this time."

With a shrug I tell her, "Put a helmet on then."

It takes us very little time to find where she is at, Hekate's storm is raging over top their building. We stop the bikes well outside of the walls of the compound, the hail storm ending as we do. They are going to need a new roof on every one of those buildings. Unfortunately, the end of the hail storm has also allowed them to venture outside. Bettina takes this opportunity to say, "I can shield us all, for a time. Depending on how many times you get hit. Each hit takes energy. So, we should avoid that, but I can probably keep us all shielded through five or six hits each, roughly."

Knox looks at Malic who says, "Don't bother with shielding us unless we falter. Keep yourself and Dagma shielded, you two are a lot less... able to withstand being shot without severe effects."

Dagma chuckles, "He's saying we die a lot easier than they do. You just keep us shielded. We'll keep an eye on them and if they stay down we'll go help them up."

Looking at the compound I see they have gathered themselves into defensible positions. "We should probably try to distract them some with our speed."

Chance says, "Yes. Ladies, do you want one of us to stay with you?"

Dagma smiles, "You're a sweet boy Chance, go and let me do my work."

I have suspicions about what she is planning to do but, that isn't my concern right now.

I take off running, and I hear the sound of guns being fired even as I stay close to the wall. Little bits of stone hit me, but no bullets I think. Then I get behind a set of men crouching behind a concrete planter.

They are spinning toward me even as I get to them, knocking the guns out of their hands. One falls before I can touch him again, the other screams as I throw him at the wall.

A bullet catches me in the arm as I turn, the men behind a vehicle and peering out at me. Running to the vehicle I grab the bottom edge and lift it, letting it tip over on anyone to slow to move in time. Walking around the vehicle I nearly get shot in the face by the one guy that didn't get caught under the vehicle. I pick up a rock and toss it to the other end of the vehicle, stepping out to catch him unaware I find that he is already dead. Then I see

Dagma walking past. I watch as a man steps out, gun in hand and she just gestures at him. The man falls to the ground, dead. Fuck, I feel a little extraneous now.

Walking a little faster till I fall in step with her I ask, "How long can you keep this up?"

She smiles, "I could probably do this to the end of time to these people. I get some energy every time I," she pauses to make the same gesture at another man, "every time I do that."

Knox speaks up from behind us, "Fuck. Dagma, let me know if I'm pissing you off. Before it comes to this. Shit."

She laughs, "You boys just keep my daughter happy and as safe as is possible. Maybe get rid of these people? I don't know the answer here. I just have a feeling that things will continue to escalate if we don't do something more permanent about them."

We are at the door now, Malic and Knox step in front of Dagma. I open the door as I tell her, "I agree. We need to get rid of the entire organization."

Seventeen

Valdís

All I can think as Eirene slaps me is that it's a damn shame they didn't wreck when I managed to flatten their tires. Physically, everything is still more than a little wonky, but my magic is getting better. The men holding me shuffle me into a room and tie me to a post. I look around as they walk away and I see twelve women in a circle chained to the floor. There is a man standing behind each woman. Oh no. No. It can't be. They can't do this.

My heart starts racing as the same old man from before walks over to me. Oh goddess no. He brings a hand up and runs a finger along my cheek. I turn my head and bite the hell out of him. There is blood in my mouth when he finally gets his finger back and I spit it at him. One of the guards that helped him hits me so hard my head hits the post behind me and I see stars. More blood in my mouth but at least this time it's mine. I spit it out on the floor, I know my kings are coming for me. The scent of my blood will only help them find me. If I have my way that old man will still be here when they do find me.

It makes me smile to think of them killing that old man. Until I hear them start the ceremony and my blood suddenly turns to ice in my veins.

I hope my kings get here soon. I can't do my magic tied up like this and I don't have the strength to break free of these ropes.

~

Eirene

I know her goddess is watching and that means those damnable kings are on their way. Probably not far behind. I need to get out of here. When the men take Valdís into that room I keep going. The men that aren't dealing with her follow me along with the lords. I ask the man next to me, "Is there a back way out of here?"

He looks puzzled as he says, "Yes, take a right here. Why?"

Taking the right I tell him, "Those creatures that ate so many of your men are on the way here for that girl right now. I slapped her to verify that her goddess is watching. If she's watching," we come to a cross hall and he gestures to continue forward, "that means they are coming. I intend not to be here when they arrive. Do I have family somewhere?"

He replies, "No. You and your daughter are the last of your line. It is amazing how young you look, considering what your age must be."

"It's an effect of that island. It slows aging a lot. Are we nearly to the exit?"

He nods, "We are. Their are other organization strongholds, and once you are recognized as the heir, you have an inheritance. They have held it in trust for you. Considering as our God has already said you are her, I don't think there will be much problem getting that sorted. Either way, they will keep you safe until it is."

He opens a door to the outside and I step through, eager to leave this place. The rain is gone completely, and I see more vehicles back here, along with a gate. Excellent. We won't even need to pass by them. "Let's go there. And be quick about getting away from here, before those damned Atlanteans catch up."

Ingemar

I follow closely as Eirene leads the way through this place. I need to figure out how to keep from being put in a cage again or left to be killed by the kings. I hear Eirene telling the guards that we need to leave for that very reason and I make certain to keep my head down and not trail behind.

She speaks freely and the guard tells her that she is royalty and has an inheritance. Fuck me.

Maybe I can become a part of her entourage. I'll fetch her damn slippers if it will keep me alive. We step outside and I see the vehicles. I am going to offer to swear fealty to her, better to be a subject than a prisoner.

I'll talk to the others, they can join in if they like. Regardless, I will do what I must to stay alive. Being an Atlantean lord doesn't mean shit here.

Eighteen

CHANCE

I can smell her. My feet have me moving toward the scent of her before I make the decision to go that way. I can feel Gage on my heels, I know he smells it too. She is bleeding. Somewhere in this building is the person that made her bleed and I am going to find that person. We get to the door and I open it slowly for her sake though I want to kick it across the room. I hear them chanting some ritual and my vision zeroes in on Valdís as the old man from before puts his hand on her chest over her heart.

Valdís looks like she is going to be sick as she cringes from his touch. Suddenly I am across the room and snatching that old man away from her. Grabbing the hand he touched her with I tear it off and toss it to the ground. The old man screams and his screams are music to my ears. I don't want Valdís to be ill for watching me tear this trash apart so I drag him out of the circle. As I go I see the strangest thing. It looks like the women's souls were being pulled into the men behind them, but as soon as I drag him out of the circle everything snaps back into place and the men fall down, looking pretty damn dead.

Good. Less to deal with when I need to focus on these screams. Lifting him up before me to look him in the eyes I pause as he starts begging, "Please don't kill me! I only did what I was told! Don't kill me! She's just a witch! No witch is worth killing a man over!"

I laugh at him, "She is worth ten of you and me. Now I'm going to make you scream till I can't smell her blood on you any more. You won't touch her or anyone else ever again."

The old man starts screaming before I finish speaking. So rude.

~

Gage

Time slows to a crawl as Chance crosses the room and snatches the old man away from her. Guards start running into the room as Chance rips off the hand the old man had on Valdís and I run to her. The ropes they used to tie her are thin and they are easily cut by my nails. Knox and Malic are laying waste to the guards, there are screams coming from everywhere. Holding her up I start to turn and see a man take aim at her. I spin to put myself between her and the bullet. It stings like hell but it will be fine. I glance back when I don't feel another shot and I see Dagma standing behind me, the man dead on the floor even as she gestures at another man. Bettina seems to be maintaining the shield, with a hand on Dagma. I lay an unconscious Valdís at their feet so gently. A pause as I brush her hair out of her face before I stand and step back from her.

Time is suddenly back to normal speed and I intercept a man running at the women protecting my Valdís and bring him up to feed, tearing into his throat. Tossing his body away I go for the next man, holding a perimeter around my queen.

Nineteen

Valdís

Everything went black when Chance took the old man out of the circle. Gage is laying me down at Dagma and Bettina's feet as I start to come to. I feel him brush my hair out of my face. Then he backs away and I open my eyes fully. Everything is chaos and blood. I sit up very carefully, and stand slowly, I don't know how far out the shield extends. Scanning Dagma and Bettina I realize they are both nearly drained. Even with the burst of energy Dagma gets from stopping those lives, it isn't enough to maintain the shield for this long. I put a hand on each of them, refilling their depleted stores. Bettina grins and thanks me. Dagma looks back at me and I tell the two of them, "Go help the women."

Bettina says, "What about you?"

"Don't worry about me, I am feeling much better

now." That isn't entirely true, but my magic is fully online. Stepping out of the shield I put my own in place and the bullet that was flying at me stops. Time seems to stop as I look around, using my magic to make all the guns in the room unusable by heating them to red hot. Taking note of every person in the room that isn't one of us I send out a blast of magic in all directions, stunning them all. The sound of bodies hitting the floor everywhere is rather satisfying.

Time catches up to me and my world spins a little making me stumble, then Malic is there, holding me steady.

Malic

The man I was about to grab suddenly stiffens and falls to the ground. I look around the room to see that all of them have fallen. Valdís is in the middle of the circle and she stumbles a bit. I am at her side instantly, checking her, seeing bruises everywhere. "Valdís, are you ok? Fucking hell, why are there so many bruises? Are you bleeding still?"

She laughs, "I think all the fresh blood on me is from you. Maybe I should be checking to see if you are bleeding? Are you all right?"

The sound of her laugh eases something in me, something I didn't realize was wound so tight.

Knox appears next to her, "It doesn't smell like she is

bleeding. Perhaps we should leave before all her fine work wears off?"

Valdís shakes her head no, "We have to bring the women. We can't leave them here. They are witches too."

Dagma, from next to the woman she is healing, says, "I agree with Valdís. We can't leave these women here. They will only be hurt and caged again and we can't leave them to that."

Valdís starts toward them and I walk with her, keeping a firm hand on her in case she stumbles or trips over a body part. She crouches before the woman Dagma just healed and touches the metal cuff around her wrist. It falls open at her touch and the woman brings the other wrist over for her to repeat the process. We follow Dagma around the room. She heals them and Valdís sets them free. Two of the chained women couldn't be healed, they were shot during the battle. Dagma just closes their eyes, whispering a short prayer that they find their way home to Hekate and rebirth on our home island.

Twenty

KNOX

We take one of their vehicles for the women. They are fully on board about leaving with us so we just pick one that has key in it and let them all pile in while we walk to the bikes we rode here. By the time we get to them, the women have pulled up behind us and are patiently waiting for us to get going.

Valdís rides with me, and I am comforted, feeling her arms around me. The ride back to the docks is entirely too short, but I am looking forward to being home. We are an entire crowd as we walk down the docks. Dagma and Bettina leading the way back to the boat while we kings bring up the rear because none of us feels entirely comfortable being so exposed. Malic is looking around as though he lost something, maybe he is just being watchful.

We hear the guns fire before the bullets hit us. Malic

and I turn, standing as a physical shield in front of Valdís and the rest of the women. I know the shield has been put up only because I see a bullet bounce off. Then I feel a hand on my back and the itch of healing happening faster even than we usually do.

Chance and Gage are running back up the dock, toward the building the shots are being fired from.

Gage

We had relaxed entirely too much. And that is how they caught us off guard firing on us while our group moves along the dock, sitting ducks for anyone looking to kill off all of us. I look to Chance and we start running at the same time. The shooters are so focused on killing the women that they don't even notice us running up the dock and across the lot. The building they are on sits between two others and they are near the same height. Chance takes the alley to the left side and I take the one to the right.

Leaping up at one wall only springboard off it up and across to the other wall till I reach the top of the building, landing on the ledge. I see them and leap toward them. As I am flying through the air one turns and sees me, swinging his gun around to shoot me. I feel the bullet rip through my chest but worse yet, the change happens. My flight is barely slowed only now everyone will know I am one of the wolf people from the old stories. I land, paws on the man's shoulders and the first thing I do is rip his throat out. Probably a little more vicious than I need to be, but he outed me and I was not ready.

Chance took care of the other two men, breaking their necks. Which is, admittedly, a cleaner way of handling things. Much less satisfying though. Chance looks over at me and grins as he says, "Brother, I think you are taking the whole idea of doggy style too far."

I snort at him and he asks, "Can you still make the leap down? Or do you need me to carry you?"

I can't speak in this form, so instead of trying to answer I walk over to the wall at the edge of the roof and hop up on it, looking back at him. He nods, "Ok then. Let's go."

The landing doesn't feel the greatest, that bullet hasn't quite worked its way out yet and the jolt moved it a bit. Beyond that the healing just itches like mad. It takes everything in me to walk normally toward the dock and everyone I care about who didn't know until now that I have been keeping this huge secret from them. It would appear that Chance is unbothered by it, but he is more like one of my people than any of the others. I would have been more surprised if he took issue with it.

Twenty-One

Valdís

I hear the shooting start and I spin around, seeing Knox and Malic get hit with the first bullets even as Bettina throws a shield up over us. I shout, "Come to me Bettina! I'll feed your power!"

Dagma pushes past me and heals my kings while I watch in horror as Chance and Gage run toward the people still shooting at us. Bettina gets next to me and I put a hand on her, pushing power into her so those bullets don't hit anyone even as my eyes stay focused on Chance and Gage.

The shooters are so focused on trying to hit us they don't see them at first. But they hear them as they catapult themselves up the sides of the buildings to get to them on the rooftops. One man turns as Gage is leaping at him and shoots him in the chest. Gage seems to almost ripple and suddenly there is a wolf in his place. The wolf is bleeding and snarling as he lands on the man and rips out his throat. Chance hits them from the other side, breaking the necks of the two men left staring in horror at their companion's throat being ripped away by a wolf.

I watch as Chance looks over at the wolf that is Gage. He grins and says something to him. I wish I could hear what he is saying, or better yet if Gage is able to answer like that? I watch as wolf and man leap off the building, landing lightly on the pavement in front of it. The wolf doesn't even stumble. Dagma is all business now as she turns and starts hustling women to the boat. Including me. I keep turning to look at the wolf walking with Chance. Once we are all on the boat I tell Malic, "I think I could create a portal, get us off the coast of home."

Malic nods, "That would be great. Wave up at me when I can go through, I am going to the helm, if you stand at the front I will be able to see you." He plants a kiss on my lips and walks away fast. My poor, sweet king. He is going to need some help getting over all this, I think. For now, much as I am dying to go check out the wolf that is Gage, I move to the front of the boat and work the magic to create a portal.

Creating it while we are in the harbor and not going pretty fast is a lot easier. Probably helps that I am not still whacked out from the drugs they gave me. I watch as Malic steers the boat through the portal, this is the biggest portal I have ever made but I wanted to make sure the whole boat fit through it. I feel certain it would be a bad thing if the bottom of the boat were to be shaved off. Once we are fully through and I have closed the portal, my job is finished and I can go have a closer look at Gage the wolf.

I find him sitting off to himself near the back of the boat. Blood streaking his fur in various places, still it looks so soft, and thick. I want to run my fingers through it. The question is, is he going to bite me if I do? Fuck it. I'm going to ask him. Walking over slowly I kneel down in front of him, "Would it be weird if I asked to pet you?" He shakes his head, looking very solemn. "Can I pet you?" He nods, looking very regal while I drop all pretense of being anything but a crazy dog lady. I bury my hands in his fur, it is just as soft and thick as it looks, positively luxurious.

Gage

Malic is going much slower than he normally would and I appreciate it. I want to look solemn and calm but with her fingers in my fur I can't. My tongue lolls out and I can feel the wolfish grin on my face. I want to talk to her, but my throat just isn't capable in this form. All too quickly we are at the dock and getting everyone off the ship. Chance and Knox are adamant that they are taking the new witches to the keep while Malic says he needs to finish checking his boat and cleaning it before he can leave. I know what they are doing and I appreciate it. Dagma pats my head as she walks by. Chance hugs Valdís and tells her, "Just keep Gage with you. He'll keep you safe. No one is going to bother you with a giant dog covered in blood walking next to you."

Asshole. I'm not a dog. He grins down at me and for a moment I consider biting him. That would probably scare her though. Dammit.

Knox walks over and gets his own hug from her, "Chance is right. No one will bother you, and if they have need of you, I am quite certain they will be willing to wait. Go get cleaned up. Wash away all the blood. We'll all have dinner together tonight and go from there. Ok?"

She nods, "It has been a really long day. I could do with a shower. What about Malic? He isn't ok."

Chance says, "We'll stop by and make him come to dinner if he isn't already back at the castle. You are still planning to stay there tonight, right? I know you said you were this morning," he chuckles ruefully, "but it's been a long week since this morning."

She shakes her head yes, "It has been a long week since this morning. Yes. I do plan to stay at the castle still. I miss my room and all of you." She reaches down and scratches my head, "This guy has become a lot less scary while I was at the keep. And now, well, I love dogs. I never got to have one growing up and as an adult, I was afraid my stepmother would kill it to hurt me for some imagined slight."

The growl slips out, but Knox nods, "I agree, Gage. Eirene has a lot to answer for in regards to how she treated our queen."

Valdís shrugs, "It's done. I would be happy if she would just let me be now. I'll see you all in a little while, yes?"

They nod and hug her again before turning to go to the vehicle that the guards brought out to take all those that need to go to the keep. They brought a second vehicle out to take Valdís and I to the main castle. One of them holds the door open for her and she insists that I get in first. Once we are in the vehicle with the door closed she says, "Some people have opinions about animals riding in vehicles, I didn't want to take any chances. You may not know it, but I have more than an idea of how truly awful people can be, so I just don't tend to trust everyone. Including the guards. But I guess if they give you any lip you could just bite them couldn't you?"

Her fingers find my neck and she starts stroking my fur again. I would be willing to bite anyone that tried to stop me from sitting here next to her. I look over at her, moving only my eyes. She has stopped talking, lost in what appears to be unhappy thoughts as she strokes my fur. Well that won't do. I flop down across her lap, she gives an oof of surprise, "What are you doing? Are you tired? Did you need to lay down? That's right, you were shot. Are you healing ok with that? Did the bullet come out yet?" She runs her hand over my chest and her fingers find the bullet that is about half out of my skin. Her hand freezes there, she asks, "Can I pull this out? Will it help if it is out?"

Not being able to speak is damned inconvenient right now. I nod and hope she understands. It would be great if she would pull the thing out. Then the hole could close up and stop irritating me. Her fingers go back to the bullet, she is so gentle as she gets a grip on it. "Ok, here we go, last chance to stop this. I'd like it if you don't get mad about this and bite me."

I wait, holding myself as still as possible. She eases the

bullet out so gently that I barely feel a twinge. I thump my tail on the seat a few times to indicate I am pleased. She scratches my shoulder, saying, "You did so well! This is a large chunk of metal. I don't know how you have been walking around ok with this as it was getting pushed out of your body. Oh look, we're home."

I am loathe to get up off her lap though I felt the car slowing. I do sit up. And I am the first to get out after the guard opens the door. He seems disturbed but he is coping rather well so I let it pass as I turn and wait for her. She exits the vehicle and I see I have left blood all over her clothes. Oh well. She puts a hand on my neck and leaves it resting there as we walk to through the garage. The elevator ride is quick and we get to the door of the castle before anyone gives us any trouble. One of the guards says, "Ma'am, I don't know if you should be bringing big, bloody dogs into the palace. Most petitioners go in the front door too." I growl at him and he pulls a dagger out, "I'm going to need you to control your dog!"

Valdís shoved me behind her when the dagger came out and she did something with her hands, now the man is standing very still as she tells him, "You listen here, I don't know who you are and I don't give a damn! You are not going to treat anyone like this, period. For one, you have to be new here. Tell me, how many random women have you seen come out of that garage? None! That's how many! It's only witches and me! And honestly, is a lady coming out of the private garage with a giant, bloody, wolf at her side the one you want to try to flex on?" She is really winding up on this guy, and has obviously immobilized him. I sit down to watch because this is great. She is all about telling him off for drawing a dagger at me, if I could I would laugh. Then Epaphras comes through the door, out of breath and saying, "Oh hell," he draws in air like he is starved for it, "What are you doing stopping the future queen? What were you thinking? She is already queen of the witches, why would you antagonize the queen of the witches? Valdís, let him go. Whatever he wasn't thinking is gone now. He is going back to training with Narich since context clues are obviously still difficult for him."

Valdís, who had stopped telling the man off as soon as she saw Epaphras, nods. "Of course. Is my room ready? I'm sorry I didn't tell you I was coming, I got a little side-tracked after I made the decision this morning."

Epaphras smiles gently at her, "My dear, don't you worry about it at all. I had a feeling you would be brought here, whether or not you had made the choice. I was pretty certain the kings would insist upon it after the shenanigans of those Outsiders. Come along, when did you get a dog?"

She laughs, "That's no dog Epaphras, that's Gage."

His eyes bug as he looks at me. I just let a wolfish grin spread across my face. He rolls his eyes, "You know, I'm not even all that surprised. It explains all the damn fur. For years I was certain he was hiding a dog in his room somewhere. Get in here, both of you." He looks at the man still standing there, though his dagger is put away now and he looks very concerned. "You get yourself to Captain Narich, and tell him you need a lot more training because you are not picking up on things well enough. I will be seeing him within the hour to let him know just what happened here."

I follow Valdís past Epaphras, he lets the door swing closed after us and catches up to Valdís, "I'm glad you are back. They missed you. And, I am very pleased that King Gage is not frightening you any longer. I confess I am curious about the reason for the blood all over him and why he is now a dog."

Valdís interjects, "I think he prefers to be called a wolf, judging by the way his face looked when Chance called him a dog."

Epaphras sighs, "Indeed. I am sure I will be given some answers when King Gage sees fit. Until then, welcome home Valdís. Now, I am told all the kings plan to eat with you in the smaller dining room this evening. I need to go attend to some things."

"Wait," he stops and turns back to her, "um, please check on my mother and grandmothers. If they would like to come have dinner with us, I want them to have space at the table too, please."

He smiles at her, "Of course. I'll see to that now. Go clean up dear, you'll want to be free of all that blood and such when you have dinner."

~

Gage

. . .

She seems comfortable having me around her in this form so I follow her to her room. She is talking away to me as we go. I listen attentively as this is the most she has ever said to me. She tells me about the old man touching her and how it felt like her skin was trying to crawl off her body to get away from him.

It makes me wish I had the time to help Chance when he was taking that old man apart. She holds the door open for me to enter her room.

It takes all my focus to walk in calmly instead of zooming around the room like my tail is on fire. As it is, my tail is wagging ridiculously and I can't seem to make it stop.

She closes the door and starts to cross the room then stops and turns, "I am going to shower. I really do need to wash away... all of it. You can come in if you get lonely."

My brain goes into overdrive with the thought that she invited me into the shower. She knows I am a man, she remembers that, right? I don't know what to do here. Because I sure as fuck am definitely lonely for her company all the time. I hear the shower start, and the sound of her standing under the spray. I look down at the blood all over me, it would take hours to lick all this off and sadly, it won't disappear just because I shifted. Fuck it. Maybe it will rinse off and I can sit in the shower and admire her.

I pad into the bathroom and see her rinsing her hair. She has so many bruises. I need to find out who put those there. For now, I walk into the shower and sit down in front of her. Sweet Goddess but she smells amazing. Dragging my eyes up to her face is difficult but I manage.

Keeping them there as she finishes rinsing her hair is a

test of all my willpower but I manage. When she look down and see me she jumps and puts a hand on her heart, "Fucking hell Gage. Some of us can die from a heart attack. Oh my goddess, you aren't still bleeding are you?" I shake my head no and she says, "Then you need scrubbed. Hm, fur is close to hair. Shampoo it is."

She grabs a bottle and applies it liberally all over my fur. Scrubbing it in really well, and I am in heaven. Thank the goddess that my wolf body doesn't have quite the same reaction to her that the human side has. That would be incredibly awkward.

She finishes scrubbing me and steps into the spray to rinse herself first. I wait patiently and she invites me under the water, using her hands to help get the shampoo out of my fur. She has no idea how nice this feels. The wolf side of me would literally fight anyone trying to interrupt this right now. All too soon she is done and I have to roll my tongue back up in my mouth. She rinses herself one more time and turns off the water. Looking down at me she says, "If you will stay put I will get a towel and help you dry off. Also, if you plan to shake the water out of your fur I would really appreciate it if you wait till I am not inside the shower. Ok?"

She is so bloody cute. I nod my head yes and wait for her to walk out and start working on towels. I watch as she wraps herself in a bath sheet, and while she is going to the cabinet for a different towel for me I go ahead and shake my fur out quite thoroughly. She kneels in front of me and keeping a hand on each end of the towel she flips the mid section of the towel over me and pulls it back and forth across me to get my back drier. When she finishes there she pulls it around front and starts rubbing it across my chest and shoulders, before drying my face much more gently. As she takes the towel away from my face she asks, "Are you stuck this way or can you change at will?"

To answer, I shift, instantly becoming a man crouched before her. Her eyes go round and I want to take her in my arms more than anything. She isn't quite ready for that so I hold myself still and wait for her to do something. Anything. For long moments she barely even breathes. I can smell her arousal and it is testing my control, but I hold on, knowing she has to make the first move or I will terrify her once again. Her hand raises, slowly coming toward my face. She stops halfway there and whispers, "Can I touch you?"

"Yes." Please, yes. I might die if you don't. I need you to like the man more than the wolf. Please touch me. Her hand resumes its slow journey, finally touching my cheek near my temple and cupping my face. I can't help myself and my eyes close as I lean my face into her hand.

She holds her hand in place as she says, "When was the last time you were touched by anyone?"

"I don't remember." I do remember, but it was before even the fight with the monster. Before Hekate changed us.

"That won't do." She takes her hand from my face and my eyes fly open, "Come. Get up and come out here with me. My knees weren't meant to kneel on shower tile endlessly." She stands and I rise with her. She takes my hand and leads me out of the shower, through the bathroom, and across the room to her bed. Pointing at the edge of the bed she says, "Sit."

I raise a brow at that phrasing but I do as she says. She could tell me to cartwheel across the room and I would do it for her. She stands before me in the vee of my legs, seemingly oblivious to the fact that I am naked. Her scent says she isn't unaware though. The sharp peaks of her nipples through the bath sheet show her awareness as well. All that slips away though as she puts her hands in my hair, caressing my scalp, running her fingers down the back of my neck and back up again. My eyes roll up as the lids drop closed. Her warm hands go back down my neck and across my shoulders, coming back to cup my face for a moment. Her thumbs run across my lower lip to meet in the middle and then go back as she takes her hands down my neck to my chest. I hold myself so very still as she encircles me with her arms to run her hands up and down my back. My cock is pressed into her chest and I think she may be kneeling in front of me but it feels like opening my eyes would distract me from the sensation of her touching me. Her hands come back to my chest, never breaking contact with my skin as she traces a path of light and fire on my body. It feels like all the darkness of the long years is being chased away by the light of her hands on my skin. Her hands slide down my arms and back up to my chest, down to my waist. I feel her hands on my legs and my cock throbs at how close her hands are. Her hands stroke all the way down to my toes, tapping each one gently.

My breath catches as her hands start the journey back up my legs. Her hands stop at the top of my thighs. I feel her lean forward, the heat from her face alongside mine, she whispers, "May I touch the rest of you?"

I try to answer and my voice doesn't work. I clear my throat, "Yes."

She leans back and her hands move so slowly across my skin and finally circle my throbbing cock, a moan breaks free of my control and she twists her hands round as she strokes upward and I am sucking air like I forgot how to breathe. Her lips circle the head and I lose all control. Her mouth is like fire as she works it around the head and never moves away, swallowing everything. "I'm so sorry. I haven't... I never... I didn't mean to do that. It just felt so good."

She lifts her head and licks her lips, "I didn't mind. It's kind of exciting that my touch turned you on so much. What do you mean when you say you never? Never what?"

My face heats, "I, um. Hm. I never had sex. At least, well, I never let anyone touch me."

She looks up at me, taking her hands off my still very hard cock, "I need you to explain. What exactly do you mean by you never let anyone touch you."

"I didn't want just anyone to touch me. It isn't that I didn't find women attractive or that I didn't want them. I just felt weird about them touching me. Like they weren't my person. It just never felt right and the idea of putting part of me inside them was abhorrent to me. So I pleasured them and kept me to me."

"But you touched you while you pleasured them, right?"

Oh wow, I didn't think my face could feel more like it was on fire and I was wrong. "I did. It was fine for me to touch me."

She frowns, "Are you sure it was ok for me to touch you? I don't want to do anything you don't want me to do. Are you still ok with that?"

Taking her hands in mine I tell her, "I very much want you to touch me. You are my person. You, I have been waiting forever for you. For you to touch me, to finally bury myself inside you. Having your hands on me is the best feeling. I really want you to touch me as often as you like. Please don't stop touching me. I waited so long for you..."

She smiles and it's like the sun came out for me. Then she asks, "Would you like to touch me?"

"More than anything."

She stands up and with one tug releases the bath sheet and drops it to the floor. I reach slowly toward her my hands going to her hips. Pulling her closer to get those breasts in my mouth. Taking a nipple in my mouth and swirling my tongue around it as I suck it further into my mouth. Her hands go to my shoulders, her nails digging in a little. I switch to the other breast and she moans.

I wrap my arms around her body and lift her up as I stand. Turning around I step up onto the bed. I start to put her down on the bed and she wraps her legs around me, bringing my cock in contact with her hot pussy. Her nipple slips from my mouth as I moan, she rocks her hips in response. I lower us to the bed slowly, one arm holding her against me as the other keeps us from hitting the bed. She is rocking her hips, creating more heat as I lower her to the bed. Her hands roam my body and it feels amazing. I need to touch her and I slip my arm out from under her, and moving it to cup her face. She brings both her hands up to cup my face and draws me down, our lips touching for the first time. The kiss starts soft but is fast heated and demanding. Our tongues delving and exploring, then she rocks her hips and lifts slightly, pushing the head of my cock into her hot core, a groan escapes my lips as I break the kiss and bury myself in her. She cries out in pleasure and I nearly come again. It is sheer force of will that keeps me from pounding her twice and finishing. Instead I hold myself still in her, leaning back down to kiss her. She holds me close as we kiss and then her hips start rocking and I can feel the hard nub of her clit as she drags it back and forth over my pubic bone.

I am so close to coming it is all I can do to stay still and hold it in. She breaks the kiss and says, "Bite me."

"What?"

"Drink from me, it feels amazing when one of you drinks lightly from me and I will come all over your cock."

With an invitation like that what am I going to do except lean down and put my teeth to her pretty neck and sink my fangs into her? Oh Goddess, she tastes amazing. Pulling my hips back just a bit I start fucking her hard and fast, within seconds she cries out with her orgasm. I can feel her pussy clenching my cock and I withdraw my teeth, I don't want to drain her. But I do want to fuck her hard and fast, make her come again when I do. I lean back, drawing my knees up to either side of her hips. Sweet Lady, she looks like a feast all sweaty and sated. I reach down with one hand and put my thumb on her clit, her eyes slowly open as I start rubbing it. She smiles and then I lean forward for leverage and start thrusting slowly. Her mouth forms an oh as she gasps and her eyes roll up. Her hands grip the sheets as I start pounding her hard and fast, struggling to hold on till she comes again. Her entire body clenches and a flood comes from her body as the spasms begin in her pussy. That is more than I can take and one last thrust has me joining her in the stars.

Twenty-Two

EIRENE

We get in two of the vehicles and are gone quickly out the back gate. As the leader drives I ask him, "Where exactly are we going?"

"To Cardinal Abel's compound. He has a bit more pull within the organization."

"Tell me about the organization. What does it do?"

"They are the stewards of the people. The ones that our God speaks to as he does not speak to those who are not sanctified in some way. For you, it is your bloodline. Your particular bloodline is holy, though I am unaware of the reason for that. It is far beyond what I need to know. I was blessed through an arduous ritual in order to increase my strength and endurance, but that must be repeated as it fades over time. The more religious parts of the organization maintain their connection differently. I am not very clear on the details of that. They don't like to talk about it with us."

"And why is the organization holding my inheritance?"

"Well that's easy, your family created the organization. On the instruction of our God, but they were created by your family. They have been holding everything in trust for a very long time. Even though a great many were certain that your line had died out during the time of the cleansing."

"The cleansing?"

"That was when your family traveled to the land of Atlantis, to cleanse our world of the Atlanteans."

"Why did my family go to do this?"

He looks at me oddly, "Did your family not teach you the history of your line?"

Looking out the window at the fast passing scenery I tell him, "We were in hiding. All I was told was that I must keep hidden the mark that their goddess set on everyone not of that land and that I must be the one to raise the family up so that we could get close enough to finish killing the kings. My mother and father always said it was best if we didn't know much about our origins because then we couldn't tell anyone by accident as children. They died before they had the chance to tell us."

"I see. I was taught that your family was sent by our God, that they were chosen to rid the world of the Atlanteans and their filth."

"What was the filth?"

"They were worshipping some false deity and living with witches. Both are punishable by death. When they banished our missionaries, after murdering some of them simply for trying to spread the good word of our God, he decided that they must go. We must cleanse our world of such creatures. Your family, being the holiest of our people, were sent with a large team. We were told by the ones that came back that your family had elected to stay to finish the mission. They told us how most of the false kings of that land were killed and only five remain."

"Well, sadly, there are still five. It hasn't been for lack of trying."

He nods, "You should get some sleep. The cardinal's compound is a long drive from here. He is in a city, far from the ocean. We can get you more clothing there too. More in the style of our people. You'll feel better."

"You might be right. Wake me before we arrive? I don't want to meet the cardinal all mussed from sleep."

He nods and I settle back into my seat. Sleep feels so far away but next thing I know the leader is touching my hand, "Queen Eirene, highness, we are at the store. Wake up."

I struggle to get my eyes open, it seems I haven't slept properly since I left the estate. When I get them open I see we are stopped, in a lot among a lot of other vehicles. There are buildings lining one side, they have lots of windows and signs up in most of them. "Where are we?"

"We are at a store. Well, a lot of stores. But we only need one or two to get you something to wear that will be better for you to meet the cardinal in."

An hour or so later we are back out to the vehicle, a bag with my old clothes and shoes being tossed into the back as we get in. One of the other men gets out of the second vehicle and brings over a couple of paper bags. Handing them to the leader he tells him, "Sir, we got food for everyone. I know this may not be quite what the lady is used to but she hasn't eaten in quite some time."

"Yes, good idea. Thank you. We'll stay here while I eat and she can take her time eating as I drive."

The man nods sharply and returns to the other vehicle. We get in the vehicle we had been using and the lead hands me a paper bag, "This won't be the best food you've ever had, but it should get you by till we finish with all of the necessary things."

The smell of the food permeates the vehicle as he speaks and I find that I am really hungry. Opening the bag I find a paper wrapped thing that smells amazing. As I unwrap it I find a sandwich with cheese and meaty bits oozing out. Taking a bite is amazing. I have never tasted anything quite so good as this. I don't know what they are doing to food here but I am going to need to have more.

The lead finishes his food and starts driving again. A few tasty minutes later my food is finished and I look over at him, "What is your name?"

He looks surprised and he says, "My name? It's Nicholas, but you don't need to worry about that. Honestly, after today you will probably never see me again. I am frequently out on assignment."

"Won't there be a protection detail assigned to me?"

"Of course. You can't wander around unprotected. Even here there are people with ill-intent. Not everyone will be happy to see the royal family return."

An idea presents itself, "Aren't you the best the organization has?"

He nods, "My team is the best, yes."

"Shouldn't the very best be who guards the royal family?"

He glances at me, but quickly returns his attention to the road, "I suppose so. I guess you'll be able to make that request. Once you have been crowned."

"I like the sound of that. Do I have a palace?"

"Yes? Right now the closest one is a museum, because there were no living heirs that anyone was aware. But it is still part of the trust so I imagine there will be very little problem with getting it ready for you."

"Hm, and have they been charging for those tours?"

"They have. I've been through a couple times."

"Oh? Is it nice?"

"It is."

"Perhaps I will continue the tours and having of a museum, with a portion of it kept as mine. After all, royalty have to expect some intrusion of privacy. If I start out with a certain amount and simply maintain it at that level, I think perhaps it will work better for me."

He nods as he makes a turn onto what appears to be a long driveway. At the end of the drive in the distance is a wall, and behind the gate I see a stern looking place. It is all white and sharp edges, mirrored looking glass. It all looks like it could slice you to ribbons for the crime of a single misstep that had you bumping one of those harsh corners.

As we stop I look at Nicholas, "I could hire you, if you think the organization wouldn't welcome your team being my guards. Would you and your team welcome that?"

He looks at me, assessing. Finally he says, "I think that we might. I warn you, our fees are high."

"If what you have told me is correct, it would appear that I have the wherewithal to pay your high fees. And it occurs to me that perhaps I want to be the one paying my security. I am willing to pay for loyalty."

"I will speak with the rest of the team. For now, let's get you in to see the cardinal."

Nicholas waits with me while the cardinal keeps us cooling our heels in a sparsely furnished waiting room. Nicholas has his men and the lords wait outside with the vehicles in order to keep it from being excessively crowded and close. An hours has passed before his man comes to escort us in to see the Cardinal.

In his office I notice he has no chairs before his desk and I know his measure. Nicholas introduces me, "Cardinal Abel, I present our recovered Queen Eirene."

Cardinal Abel raises a perfectly manicured brow, "Indeed. And did you collect the key as well?"

Nicholas nods, "I did, though it is uncertain as to whether we retain the key."

"Why is that?"

"The monsters from her land were not far behind. They entered the building as we exited through a back door. We thought it best to get the queen out since the likelihood of retaining the key was slim."

"That decision is well above your station to make. You were sent for the key, you should have stayed to ensure we retained it."

"Cardinal Abel, we were also told to bring the queen back. I chose to ensure retention of the one we could succeed in keeping."

Cardinal Abel stands, "You are not payed to decide. You and your team are relieved of your position. As for you madame, we will have you escorted to one of the nun's rooms where you may stay until we have verified your claim."

I recognize this kind of man and I smile at him, "No. Call him."

His face ripples with annoyance, "How dare you tell me no? You are not queen madame, and have no say in the matter."

"I am and I do. Call him or I will."

A bead of sweat rolls down his temple, "Call who?"

"Our God. You call him or I will. If I call him I will tell him what you attempted here today."

His skin pales and he lifts a glass of wine with a hand that trembles slightly and takes a sip. Slowly setting the glass down he says, "Very well. Let that be the test. Only a blood born royal can call him without the rituals, if he answers you then here before these witnesses I will accept that you are the queen."

"Fine." I clear my throat and call him the way he told me to as the good Cardinal Abel pales further.

He answers from nowhere and everywhere, "Yes, my dear one?"

"Forgive me for disturbing you. Cardinal Abel is unsure as to whether or not I am the Queen. He wanted to toss me in the nunnery to rot until he got around to checking. He seems... reluctant to release my property to me without further evidence."

My God appears in the room with us, everyone besides the Cardinal and myself prostrates themselves. For my part, I curtsy. I watch out of the corner of my eye as Cardinal Abel freezes. Our God advances on him, coming around his desk to stand next to him. Cardinal Abel turns to face him as he approaches. The Cardinal is visibly shaking as our God steps up next to him, "Cardinal Abel, I haven't heard from you in a very long time. I feel slighted. Like you didn't want to talk to me, your God, your reason for living."

The Cardinal drops to his knees before him, "I'm not worthy! Forgive me! I knew I wasn't worthy and I couldn't appear before you in my unworthy state."

Our God places a finger under his chin and forces him back to a standing position. Instead of removing his finger once he is standing our God forces him to his toes, "I expect all of the royal holdings to be released to Eirene immediately. Everything. And you will perform the ritual daily until I feel you have redeemed yourself. We will speak further about the rest of your punishments during the ritual. For now, everyone here is witness that this woman Eirene Potentus is the queen of my lands. You will treat her as such and know that I have my eye on her."

He disappears after his proclamation and the Cardinal stumbles, catching himself on his desk. He grabs the glass and drinks it down. Setting it back down with still shaking hands he says to one of his men, "Get the papers and ready the ceremony. She will be crowned tonight." He looks directly at me now, "May I invite you to refresh yourself in one of our guest suites while we make the preparations?"

"Yes. I have people outside waiting my presence as well, they must be given suitable accommodations so that they may refresh themselves as well. Both my guests and my guards."

The Cardinal looks sharply at me, "What guards?"

"The only thing you need concern yourself with is following our God's orders. Or should I call him back? I am certain he would be very happy to be called back so soon after his last visit."

"No! No, that won't be necessary. Yes, your team and your guests will be made comfortable."

I smile, "Excellent, Nicholas will stay with me."

The Cardinal grimaces and nods, "Very well. Take her to a guest suite. Nicholas, I would like to speak with you before you join our Queen."

Nicholas smiles, "I'm sorry Cardinal Abel, but as the Queen is now my employer and has requested that I stay with her, I will not be able to accommodate your wishes."

Cardinal Abel flushes a very unbecoming shade of red, "I see. I will not forget this."

I turn and smile at him, "What you should keep in mind Cardinal Abel, is that you are not the ruling authority. You are also not his only Cardinal. I have a close relationship with our God as you will find during your punishments. He will hear all about you. I'll see you at the coronation. He'll be watching."

The good Cardinal's face is nearly purple as I follow his man out of the room. The man guides me through the halls with Nicholas right on my heels into a spacious suite. It isn't their nicest I think, but it doesn't matter. Once in the room I wait for the man to leave and turn to Nicholas, "There are news places here, yes? Papers that come out daily? That sort of thing?" Nicholas nods, "Excellent. We must get in touch with them and ensure that they are here for the coronation."

He grins, "That is a very good idea." He pulls an item out of his pocket and taps it a bit before putting it to his ear and having a conversation. He pauses and looks to me, "Your highness, would you be willing to answer questions for a number of them for a few minutes after the coronation?"

"I would. And, once I am home we can choose one of them to give an exclusive interview."

While he is still speaking there is a knock on the door, he rushes to answer it, and allows one of the Cardinal's men entry into the room. The man looks to me, "Your highness, we need to go over these documents regarding your estates."

Nicholas takes the item away from his ear, and tells the man, "I have one of my men coming to this room now. He will assist the queen in going over the documents." Looking at me he says, "The man I have on the way is well versed in our legal system, being a lawyer when we are not on assignment."

I nod, "Very well, we will wait for him before we begin."

The man looks nervous, "Your highness, the Cardinal wants this done before the coronation."

I'm sure he does. I can't wait to see what Nicholas's man finds in these papers, "We will wait. They can't have the coronation without me." There is a tap at the door and Nicholas opens it to admit one of his men. "Oh look, we don't even need to wait, there he is."

The man swallows, "Yes. There he is."

After that we play a stupid game where the man says what a document is supposed to be and passes it over to me. I hand it to the man Nicholas called in, whose name is Edgar. Edgar reads the document and makes changes, telling us exactly what he is changing as he does so and insisting that we both sign the changes. The man tried to say he wasn't authorized to sign the changes and Edgar simply pointed out that if he was authorized to sign the documents, he is authorized to sign the changes.

The man is sweating by the time we finish. But, there are finally two sets of documents, both signed and stamped by the man. He is very unhappy and tells me that the Cardinal will not like the changes. With a smile I tell him, "I will be sure to let our God know all the details of what he tried to have done here today."

The man passes out. Just falling out on the floor. All of us are just stunned, I ask Nicholas and Edgar, "Does this usually happen?"

Nicholas shrugs, "It isn't very often that someone has the comeback that they are going to let our God know what is going on here and actually can do that. But, the press," at my questioning look he says, "our news people are piling up outside. We would like to have you go out and answer a few questions before the coronation. Let them get pictures of you and you can possibly get a feel for which one you would like to do the exclusive interview."

I look down at the outfit I bought today. It isn't the fanciest outfit I have ever owned, being no more that a skirt suit. It will have to do. "Yes. The coronation should be happening soon. I know he said later, but I feel certain that with the press? Is that what you called them?" He nods, "I feel certain that with them watching the good Cardinal Abel will want to get it done as soon as possible."

Nicholas chuckles, "I imagine he will at that."

As we suspected, the Cardinal Abel suddenly was ready to hold the coronation moments after I stepped out the front door to speak to the press. When he sent a man out to collect us for the coronation there was an immediate clamor from the press people that they needed to be in there to record this for the people.

They are allowed, with great reluctance on the part of Cardinal Abel's staff. With the press watching the coronation moves along quickly. I don't know if they have crowns stored at all of the compounds belonging to the organization, but they pulled one out here and set on my head a crown dripping in blood red stones. Right after Cardinal Abel sets the crown our God's voice booms out over the crowd, "It is done! The rightful ruler of our land is returned. Let our people rejoice! A new and better age is upon us!"

The press people cheer as Cardinal Abel's bowels make some dreadful sounds and he quickly excuses himself. I answer a few more questions and tell the press, "I will give one exclusive interview very soon. Right now, I must go find one of my homes. Please do give your cards to one of my men and we will be in touch. Thank you!"

I am over the moon as I wave goodbye to these people taking my picture over and over. Nicholas and some of his men keep me surrounded as they walk me out to the vehicle. I see the lords are already outside, standing next to the other vehicle. Once everyone is loaded and Nicholas is driving us away from the compound I ask, "Do you know where my properties are?"

He nods, "Yes. One is not far from here, we are going to that one now. Edgar made sure that the people running it are aware you will be there and they are waiting on your arrival so that they can let you in and see what will happen going forward."

"I confess, with you there Edgar, I did not read any of the documents. How many properties do I own?"

From the back seat he says, "It would appear you own twenty estates and various businesses."

"I see. Am I quite well off?"

Edgar chuckles, "You could say that. We'll get you to the money people listed here tomorrow and you can go over things with them."

"Excellent. Then I can get to work on how we are to get possession of that key again."

Twenty-Three

Valdís

Another, much faster, shower later and we take ourselves out to meet with everyone for dinner. It is the best to be here with my kings. Malic scoops me up as I walk into the dinning room, hugging me tightly to his body, "I have missed having you here at home. I'm quitting the king bit immediately if you leave again."

"I will try to refrain from leaving again for so long."

"Good," he says as he sets me down.

Knox is next but he simply takes my face in his hands and kisses my forehead before going to his seat. Chance holds out his arm and once I slip my hand into the crook of his elbow he escorts me to my chair. He takes the chair next to me as Gage sits across from me. Having all of them here makes the empty chairs so much more noticeable.

I can only imagine how much pain it caused them when

their brothers died. How frightened they must have been when I was taken. Looking at my kings I realize I have to put an end to this. Hekate said I am the key, well maybe I am not just the key to the magic. What if I can become more? Become the key to stopping this war between Hekate and this other God that wants her power so bad? Could it be possible that she followed this path for just that? So I would come to the conclusion that there must be another way? I have to try, I can't let them continue to suffer. I know they aren't going to want to even think about this, but I feel certain that we must. "I think we need to put a stop to this."

Gage looks stricken and my other kings don't look much better when Malic says, "I think maybe we need some context?"

"The war? The continual attempts to control me?" As their faces relax I realize what they must have thought, "Oh! No! Not this! I don't want to stop this, at all. I love each of you in your own way and I don't want to stop this," I gesture around at all of us, "this is good."

Everyone seems to be starting to breathe again and I am sorry to have worried them. Knox's brow draws down, "What do you mean put a stop to this? Did you have something in mind?"

Malic shakes his head, "I don't think we have the power to go against a God. That would put us all at risk in ways I don't like to think about."

Chance shrugs, "We are already at risk. He wants every one of us dead." He waves a hand at the empty seats, "That is why they are all gone. He isn't going to stop for having lost a few times. And you may not have heard what Hekate said on the boat, but it's been playing in my mind since I heard it. I know you didn't hear it Valdís, but she said that his power, his ability is making monsters. The monster we fought was made by him. He is still making monsters, only now they look like people. Like people."

Holy shit. Monsters that look like us? I mean, Eirene makes so much more sense now. Malic shakes his head no again, "That is exactly why we can't go up against him. We barely managed to kill the large monster he sent. Now he is making smaller monsters, who knows how many he has made? We could be overwhelmed by sheer numbers."

The conversation is not going where I had hoped. The guys all have opinions and not a lot of give. It seems to be split with Knox and Chance on the side of, we are getting attacked anyway may as well go on the offensive. Malic and Gage seem to be united except Gage wants to kill off the organization?

"Wait, Gage, what did you say?"

"I said that they are much easier if we pick them off one at a time. I have been hunting the higher ups in the organization for years. I just haven't been in any rush. So I took my time and made a game of it. But if we were to start picking them off faster, that would weaken him."

Knox says, "I don't understand? How would that weaken him?"

Gage says, "If I understand correctly, their God feeds off of their worship of him. Only a select few pass that worship to him. The organization is like a repository, they collect it for him. So if the feeding tube is gone he is bound to get weaker, right?"

Chance leans forward putting his elbows on the table, "It makes sense. If he can be weakened enough perhaps we could trap him, or something?"

Malic throws his hands up, "Trap a God? Do you hear the words coming out of your mouth?"

Gage sips his wine, "I think he has an idea. But I think we should ask Hekate if we can kill him. She seems unable to do things, but perhaps she can continue to feed us information."

Setting my glass down I raise my voice a bit, "Excuse me, gentlemen." They are slow to quiet, but they do and when they are all focused on listening I say, "I think Gage may be on to something. We should talk to Hekate. She sees and knows a lot more than any of us. Also, we aren't alone in this. Even if Hekate can't give us information, we have the rest of the witches. These women are fierce, they are fighters. For a great many of them, they are only alive still because they fought to stay alive. I think in your desire to protect you forget that you are not the only ones capable of protecting."

The silence at the table is incredibly loud after what I said until Chance smirks, "If the two K's are teaching them we are all in trouble."

Knox puts his head in his hands, "Oh Goddess, please don't let them train all the witches."

Laughing I tell him, "Of course not. Dagma is teaching them," I see a lot of nervous swallows around the table. "Ah, she showed you what she could do besides heal." They nod in sync, "I think you have nothing to worry about. She, it isn't something she wants to use and if she uses it, well... it is always going to be because she has no other choice."

Chance opens his mouth but it snaps shut as a roar of anger drowns out anything he might have said. Knox looks at Malic, "I believe that will be Vincent."

Vincent

I hate going home. The monastery is cool. Quiet. Calming in all the ways I need since I figured out that our Goddess lied to us about the queen.

The queen that would have saved us all.

It was nothing more than a dream, a fairytale to convince us to do her bidding. I hate her for it. Hate her for the lie. Hate her because I wanted it so badly. Wanted the queen so badly.

Now, here I am, on my way back to Atlantis to save it once again. I would just as soon that it had sunk into the ocean amid earthquakes and fire as the water swallowed it whole the way she made them all think had happened.

Instead, I have had increasingly urgent messages from Malic as problems multiply in our homeland. I put off leaving the monastery as long as I could. The Monks were not sad to see me go. I think they may have figured out my nature, I stayed there too long. I'll have to find a different one to stay at when I leave again. Unless, maybe, perhaps I can die in a battle. It appears that war is coming to our land. Perhaps it will be my time. My time to have the peace of the end.

That would make this trip home worth it.

Slowing my boat as I draw near to the cove we dock in, I see all four of my brother's boats in dock. I haven't seen that in hundreds of years. I haven't seen all of them at once in as long. They are why I came here at all, just to help them. I come here to take my turn at ruling just to take some of it off of them. They still care. I would let this place burn.

I didn't let Epaphras know exactly when I would arrive, so while he has my room ready, he doesn't have anyone out here to help me to moor the boat. It's better this way, I prefer the challenge of doing it all myself. As I work I smell something on the breeze. Something... enticing. I don't want to be enticed by anything here!

Every whiff of that scent stokes the fire of my rage. It takes me twice as long to get the boat moored because I keep making stupid mistakes. Even the damn garage has traces of it. Grabbing a bike I take the tunnels at speeds that would destroy the tunnel if I wreck. It's tempting, for the possibility of ending it all. But my brothers need me. For them I slow the bike. For them I avoid the walls. For them I struggle to keep from losing my mind as the scent gets stronger.

The garage at the other end feels close and crowded with the scent. It brings feelings to the surface, feelings I crushed and put away. It took so long to stop feeling them. Why? Why is some damn scent bringing all this up?

By the time I get to the top level, my rage is at the

boiling point. The guards there snap to attention but stay silent. I haven't often been in a good mood coming home and over the years they have learned that it's better not to speak to me.

Walking into the castle I can't smell anything but this scent. What the hell is this scent? It's driving me crazy. I see Epaphras ahead of me and call out to him. He jumps and turns, coming to stand before me, "Yes, sire?"

"What is that fucking smell?"

He flinches, "If recent history is anything to judge by, the smell is Valdís."

"Valdís? Who the fuck is that?"

Sweat beads his brow, "That is the woman that all of your brothers are currently involved with, sire."

"Involved? All my brothers are involved with the same woman how?"

"They are all romantically involved with her."

He takes a step back as I process this information. It can't be. It isn't possible. She can't be the one after all these years. "Where does she stay?"

Epaphras backs away slowly, whispering, "In the queen's suite."

The roar that comes from my throat sounds completely inhuman and I don't care. "Did you let her in there?" He shakes his head no, "Where is she now?"

"The private dining room with your brothers."

My heart feels like it will beat out of my chest even as I am frozen in fear. What if it isn't her? What if it is? What if she is the Queen? The halls seem to go on forever as I summon the control to walk to the dining room they are in.

The scent is intoxicating, maddening. Stopping outside the door with hands clenched into fists I don't know what I should be hoping for here. Should I hope that she, our queen, has finally arrived? Or should I hope that this scent is just some awful torment we must endure? I don't know. I do know I can't stand out here forever. I can hear the murmurs of their conversation through the closed door. There is a woman's voice in there.

Just open the door Vincent, you can handle this. My vision narrows to my hand turning the knob and time seems to move at a snails pace as even more of that delicious scent permeates the air around me. Then the door is fully open and I see the five of them sitting around the table. They put her in the queen's chair. It really might be her. I could cry with relief or anger that it took so long or something. I want to say something but I feel frozen again. How can I be so terrified of one woman? I can't do this right now. I'm not ready. Spinning around I leave the door standing open as I walk back the way I came and out to the gardens to hopefully clear my head.

Valdís

"Well, that went better than it could have considering the roar."

Gage looks puzzled, "Why did he smell like he was afraid? Vincent isn't usually afraid of anything."

Malic looks over at me, "It's her. He's afraid of her."

Knox laughs, "What an odd bunch we all are. The

woman we have waited centuries to find scares the hell out of all of us when we first find her. Or shuts off our reasoning centers."

Gage chuckles, "It was just at first, it was a little overwhelming. Other sides may have had a little more control over my actions than has ever happened before. I wouldn't have hurt you," his eyes meet mine, "you know that now, right?"

"I do. I have no fear of any of you these days. In fact, if you will excuse me gentlemen, I think maybe I will go find Vincent."

Chance asks, "Would you like some company?"

"Do you think that would make it easier for him?"

Chance shrugs, "Probably not."

"Then no," I stand and lean over to kiss the top of his head, "I will go and give him the opportunity to talk to me without the pressure of you all watching." Leaving the dining room I follow my nose. I can smell Vincent as strongly as I could all the others. As I can still smell the others. The effect of the scent calms once we have mated but the scent is always there. His scent leads me to the gardens. My trusty guards have followed me, as they do if I am not in the company of my kings, "I am going to find King Vincent. I know you need to stay with me and I am fine with that. But when I find him could you hang back a little extra for privacy reasons?"

They nod and I push through the doors with them following close behind. Vincent's scent is easy to pick out among the flowers. He smells of parchment and earth and longing. I didn't know that longing had a scent till now, but that is the only description that feels accurate. I find him where the jasmine and wisteria are growing over lattice and arches. My guards hang back like I asked them to do and I step into the clearing, "Vincent?"

He doesn't turn, doesn't look at me. "Shouldn't you be off hiding from the big, bad king who couldn't even speak to you?"

His voice sounds raw and I want to go to him, but I don't know whether he would want that. "Honestly, so far your reaction to my presence has been a lot less excited than the others. Needing to go have a moment alone or not want an audience, that's pretty understandable."

"Oh? What were my brother's reactions to you?"

Leaning against one of the supports for the lattice, "Well Knox started out with the I want you but you are not for me and I am going to be a miserable shit about it. At the same time he couldn't let me leave because people were trying really hard to kidnap and possibly kill me. Then Malic came along, he seemed to think it was my fault he was so attracted to me and he was an utter asshole who made me cry. Then Chance came home, he was certain I was plotting the downfall of the kingdom so he followed me everywhere, even to the point that he was hiding in my room when I created a portal to go rescue other witches. He didn't really think that through though as when I realized he had jumped through behind me, I just closed the portal." I think he huffed a little laugh there, maybe this is working? "And Gage, oh Gage. Gage has been secret keeping all this time and when he first arrived home we all were pretty sure he was about to try real hard to murder me.

Since then, we found out that he has reasons for it and he has that under control now. But the surprise of me did funny things to him that he wasn't expecting."

Vincent turns to look at me. It is dark but the moon is out, so I can see his face, if not all the smaller details of it. "What has Gage been hiding all this time?"

"Nope. I'm not telling his secrets. We found out because we were there. I know he doesn't plan to keep it secret but it is still his story to tell. What story would you to tell?"

He takes a step toward me. It's a single step but I'll take it. "I could tell a story about a king that sees the one thing he has longed for and doesn't know what to do now that it is possibly in front of him."

"It's a hard thing to wait so long for something. Now that you are here, and maybe a little more ok with talking to me, I was given a sort of assignment. I think you should maybe sit down for this though. I understand from the others that it is a bit disorienting at first and hitting the ground still doesn't feel the greatest."

"What have you got to tell me that would do that?"

"Her name."

"Her name?"

"The name of our Goddess. She seems to have caused you all to forget a number of things and I think the combination of that and some other things accounts for the disorientation."

He shakes his head no, "I'll take the fall if that is how it goes."

With a shrug I tell him, "That's your choice. Hekate."

His eyelids close, a slow drifting down as he seems to sway in a breeze only he feels. I wait, ready to use my magic to keep him upright but he stands there still and silent. When his eyes open, he looks enraged. His face twists and I don't know what to do. No one else came back infuriated after they heard her name.

"How could she?"

"I'm sorry, I don't know exactly what you mean?"

He snarls at me, "Of course you don't! You're just the damn messenger!"

"Ok then, it seems you might need to process. I'll leave you to sort your feelings."

As I turn to leave he is suddenly in front of me, I hear one of my guards take off for the castle. I know there isn't much time before my kings show up as Vincent says, "So what? You think you will let me sort my feelings and suddenly I will accept you? Confirm you as queen? Is that what you are waiting for? You are no better than the rest of them! All looking for a better life full of riches and no concept of what it takes to rule! No concept of the responsibility of it all! You may be worse though, being Hekate's little puppet! Dutifully dispensing her name where you're told to do so." He sneers at me, "Do you get off on watching people fall to the ground helpless when you say her name?"

And just like that I'm mad. A twitch of my fingers and Vincent can't move anywhere. I take a step back because I don't want him in my face like he was, "I don't appreciate your behavior. It is uncalled for on my part. I am trying to do the best I can with a lot of things that were forced on me. You know nothing about me and your statements are incredibly insulting. You can stand here until I feel like letting you go. Perhaps the fresh air will clear your mind. Good evening."

"You can't leave me standing here like this!"

"Who exactly do you think will stop me?" My kings come running to us then, stopping as they see Vincent struggling to move.

"So, what's going on here?"

I look to Knox and answer his question, "King Vincent was being very rude and he invaded my personal space. Now he can stay in his own personal space and think about why he shouldn't be so rude to people he doesn't even know."

Chance giggles, "Oh shit, what did he say to piss you off like that?"

"Awful things. I'm going inside. You gentlemen have a nice night."

Gage turns, "I'll go with you."

Chance says, "I'm staying to give him shit. I'll see you in the morning."

Malic shoves a hand through his hair, "Dammit Vincent, what the hell were you thinking?"

As I walk away I hear Vincent snarling at him, "Make her let me out of here!"

Knox chuckles, "If I were you I would be grateful that she didn't hang me by my ankles a fair way up in the air. What did you say to her?"

About the Author

Rhiannon writes steamy paranormal romance. She is an avid reader of many authors in a variety of genre though she tends more toward paranormal.

She has three former pound puppies that she dotes on and three daughters that she adores.

Rhiannon has lived in multiple states though she is currently residing in North Carolina. Wandering, witching, and reading with her puppies and husband are what she does when she isn't writing.

To learn about what is happening in Rhiannon's world and get loads of pupper cuteness, sign up for the by using the QR code below to visit my website.

The Daughter of the Moon series-

Selena Rose, Daughter of the Moon Book 1

Thorns of the Rose, Daughter of the Moon Book 2

Heart of the Rose, Daughter of the Moon Book 3

The Fate's Chronicles series

A Vampire's Fate

A Vampire's Treasure

A Vampire's Dream

A Vampire's Chase

A Vampire's Fight

Fated for Halloween - only available via email signup

The Belancore Witches of North Carolina series

Witchy Ever After

A Witchy New Year

My Witchy Valentine

Sin series

Sin on a Dark Knight

Sin on a Broken Heart

Sin on a Burning Heart

Sin on a Vengeful Heart

The Vampire Kings Series

Mercy of the Vampire King

Shame of the Vampire King

Pursuit of the Vampire King

Prey of the Vampire King

Reign of the Vampire King

Coming Soon

Love and Vampires Series

Olivia's Fall

Olivia's Prison

Olivia's Flight

Olivia's Family

Warriors of the Old Gods

A Dream of Blood

A Dream of Wolves

A Dream of Stone

A Dream of Ravens

A Dream of Bones

www.ingramcontent.com/pod-product-compliance
Lightning Source LLC
Chambersburg PA
CBHW030803190726
48285CB00003B/995